# ANACONDA
# AMBUSH

# ANACONDA
# AMBUSH

## Justin D'Ath

A & C Black • London

For Arielle Suhr and Tyler Postle, the two newest
members of the October 4 Club

First published in the UK in 2011 by
A & C Black Publishers Ltd
36 Soho Square, London, W1D 3QY

www.acblack.com

First published in Australia by
Penguin Group (Australia)
A division of Pearson Australia Group Pty Ltd

ISBN 978-1-4081-2644-8

A CIP catalogue for this book is available from the British Library.

Printed and bound in Great Britain
by TJ International Ltd, Padstow, Cornwall.

# 1
# PIRANHAS!

The animal was perfectly camouflaged in the leafy wall of jungle that pressed right down to the river's edge. Even Caesar, our Brazilian boatman, didn't see it. But Uncle Shaun had spent most of his life studying plants – a five kilogram herbivore pretending to be a clump of leaves didn't fool him for one second.

'Look, Sam – a sloth.'

All I saw was jungle.

'Where?'

'In that big kapok tree leaning out over the water.'

'Which one's that?' I asked. The trees all looked the same to me.

Uncle Shaun turned to the boatman. 'Can you take us over there, Caesar?'

It wasn't until we were right underneath the tree that I finally spotted the sloth. It dangled upside down from a branch about three metres above our peke-peke, the long motorised canoe that had brought us all the way up the Matatoro River from the Amazon. Now I understood why I hadn't seen it earlier.

'It's *green*!' I said.

Uncle Shaun nodded. 'At certain times of year they get algae – kind of like moss – growing in their fur. Want to get a photo?'

I pulled my new camera out of its waterproof case. It was an early birthday present from my parents, who thought it would come in handy on this trip with my world-famous botanist uncle. So far we'd seen caimans (a type of alligator), capybaras (rodents the size of sheep), freshwater dolphins, giant otters, four kinds of monkey and about a million birds – but this was my first sloth. I tried to find it on the LCD screen.

'Can we go forwards a bit? There are too many leaves in the way.'

Caesar hauled sideways on the outboard motor. It had a really long propeller shaft and was hard to steer.

*Bump!*

The front of the peke-peke hit a submerged log and began to spin around in the current. Uncle Shaun grasped an overhead branch to steady us. But the branch was hollow; it snapped off in his hand. And out of its honeycombed interior came a shower of squirming brown insects.

'Fire ants!' cried Caesar. 'Look out, Mr Shaun!'

His warning came too late. Already Uncle Shaun was covered from head to foot in a blanket of fire ants. Their stings are worse than bees.

Caesar didn't hesitate. Scrambling forward, he grabbed Uncle Shaun around the middle, lifted him out of his seat and rolled over the side with a huge, two-man splash.

It all happened really quickly. One moment three of us were in the canoe, next moment there was just me and a swarm of fire ants. They looked pretty revved up. Now that Uncle Shaun was gone, the big, angry ants were rushing about looking for something else to attack.

Me.

I'm allergic to insect stings. One jab from their venomous stingers sends me into anaphylactic shock: my throat swells up, my heart slows down, I can't breathe. That's why I always have an EpiPen with me. I'd brought *three* on this trip (Mum insisted), but they were in my pack. And it was in the middle of the canoe. Covered in fire ants.

'Mr Sam! Mr Sam!'

Two heads bobbed in the milky brown water about 30 metres away. It surprised me how far the peke-peke had drifted in the few seconds I'd been distracted by the ants. Caesar was waving madly at me as he and Uncle Shaun struggled towards the riverbank.

'Stop the boat, Mr Sam!'

I switched my gaze to the rear of the canoe. The motor was still running and the peke-peke was pointed downstream. No wonder it was moving so fast.

'Do a U-turn!' yelled Uncle Shaun.

It was a good plan. But the motor was at one end of the peke-peke and I was at the other. Between us was Fire Ant Central.

What was that tickling sensation?

I looked down.

Shishekbab! A fire ant had sneaked down to my end of the canoe and climbed into my sandal. Too scared to move, I watched it scurry across my bare ankle, crawl onto the heel strap of my sandal and plunge its venomous stinger into the leather.

I quickly raised my foot and shook it over the side.

'*Hasta la vista!*' I called as the current swept the ant away.

I'd been lucky – the ant had stung my sandal, not me. But how much longer was my luck going to last? About 100 more fire ants were closing in.

It was time to abandon ship.

'Sam, what are you *doing*?' Uncle Shaun yelled as I rose to my feet.

'The boat's full of fire ants,' I called back. 'If they sting me, I'm toast!'

Uncle Shaun was scrambling onto the riverbank about 60 metres away. By the time his next words reached me, I'd already jumped.

'Watch out for piranhas!'

# 2
# BLOOD AND BONES

There *were* piranhas in the Matatoro River. We'd seen heaps of them over the past four days. Caesar had caught one on a wire fishing line the previous evening. When he took the piranha off the hook, it bit the handle of his fishing knife so hard it left teeth marks in the wood.

I imagined what those teeth would do to human flesh.

Piranhas have the worst reputation of any fresh-water fish. If a shoal goes into a feeding frenzy, they can strip the carcass of a deer or a capybara in a matter of minutes. All that's left is a patch of bloody water and a pile of bones on the river bottom.

But unless they're starving or there's already blood in

the water, piranhas rarely attack humans.

I'd be OK.

Or so I thought until the river closed over my head.

*Thwop, thwop, thwop . . .*

That's what a boat's propeller sounds like underwater. I'd heard it once before (when I was nearly run down by smugglers in the Coral Sea) so I recognised the sound even though I couldn't see the propeller in the murky brown water.

It'll go past me, I told myself as I bobbed back to the surface.

I was wrong.

When I'd jumped off the peke-peke, my feet had pushed the low, rudderless craft into a spin. It spun out of control, swinging its extended propeller like an underwater brush-cutter.

Straight towards me!

There wasn't time to dive. There wasn't time to get out of the way. All I could do was put my hands up to protect my head and chest.

*Thwop, thwop, thwop . . .*

*BUMP!*

I half expected to lose all my fingers. But instead of striking the propeller, my hands hit a smooth iron bar. And grabbed hold.

Peke-pekes are designed for rivers where there are lots of underwater snags and sandbars. The propeller doesn't hang below the stern like in a normal boat, it sticks out behind on the end of a three-metre shaft. The turning part of the shaft is housed inside a hollow metal bar, like a pipe. That's what I grabbed.

I didn't lose any fingers, but now my toes were in danger. The whirling propeller blades created suction, dragging my feet towards them.

*Thwop, thwop, thwop . . .*

In two seconds I'd be chopped-up piranha bait! Drawing my knees up against my chest, I hauled myself, hand over hand, along the metal bar until I was almost under the peke-peke's stern. Now I was safe from the propeller, but I was still in a fix. The peke-peke was heading downriver again. I couldn't let go because I'd be sucked back into the propeller. And I couldn't climb aboard because it was overrun with deadly fire ants.

OK, I would just have to hang on until the peke-peke

either ran out of petrol, or ran aground.

But there was a third possibility. One that I hadn't considered. I should have thought of it, but when Uncle Shaun first spotted the sloth, everything else completely slipped from my mind.

Including how we'd spent the previous three hours.

That's how long it took to haul the peke-peke out of the river, take all our gear out of it, carry everything (including the peke-peke) up a steep, slippery, vine-entangled cliff face, then reload the peke-peke and slide it back into the river.

Why had we gone to all this bother?

Because a peke-peke won't go up a waterfall.

But it will go *down* one. As I was about to find out.

# 3
# THE BIG BEAST

The Matatoro River, or the Rio Matatoro as the Brazilians call it, flows down from the Guiana Highlands on the northern edge of the Amazon basin. It takes a 300-kilometre journey through some of the most remote and inhospitable jungle on the planet. In the wet season it's impossible to travel up the Matatoro because the current is too strong. In the dry season – when Uncle Shaun and I visited – you can get most of the way up in a peke-peke or a dugout canoe. But few people make the journey because you spend half your time steering your boat around rapids or hauling it, and your supplies, up waterfalls.

So far we had struggled up three small waterfalls – ranging in height from about four to six metres – and one large one of about 12 metres. It was the 12-metre waterfall that had kept us busy for most of the morning. According to Caesar, the local Indians called it the Big Beast. I can understand why. Getting up it had been a major pain.

But what took three hours to go up, took only three *seconds* to go down.

It seemed longer. Time has a way of slowing down when you think you're about to die. Your whole life flashes before your eyes.

And if your eyes are open, you see other stuff, too.

Here's what I saw: a wall of brown water, like a cliff, right next to me. A swarm of ants – *flying* ants, yet they didn't have wings – all around me. And an upside-down, flying peke-peke, right above me.

And here's what I heard: a thunderous roar so loud that I could no longer hear the flying peke-peke's motor.

And here's what I felt at the end of those three slowed-down seconds:

*SMAAAAAAAAAAAAACK!*

Every summer back at our local pool there's a dive-bombing competition. Competitors jump off the one-metre diving board and try to make the biggest splash. There's a three-metre board, but you have to be over 18 and sign a release form to use it.

I wonder what sort of form you would have to sign before they'd let you do a dive-bomb off the Big Beast? Probably a last will and testament. Because hitting the water from a height of 12 metres feels like landing on concrete. All the wind was knocked out of me and I blacked out.

At least, I *thought* I'd blacked out, until I bumped my head on something and saw stars. You don't see stars if you're unconscious. I was lying on my back on a lumpy bed of cold rocks and something was on top of me. Something too heavy to move. A deep, dull roar filled my ears and strong currents tugged at my clothing. Most of me was underwater – and under the heavy thing that was pinning me down – but my face wasn't. I could breathe. I could even move my head around. But I couldn't see anything. It was totally dark.

Perhaps I *had* been knocked out, and I'd lain

unconscious all day and now it was night-time.

I started to panic. Where were Uncle Shaun and Caesar? I knew they would come downriver looking for me, but they'd never find me in the dark. They didn't have torches. All our gear was in the peke-peke, and the peke-peke had gone over the waterfall with me.

'Help!' I shouted. But I was wasting my breath. The roar of falling water was so loud, I could barely hear my own voice.

But I could *feel* my voice. Each time I shouted, my breath blew back in my face. As if it was bouncing off something.

Curiously, I raised my head. And bumped my nose and forehead against a damp arc of wood. Suddenly I worked it out. I was under the peke-peke! It must have landed upside down on the river bottom, trapping me underneath.

I freed one arm and pushed upwards. The canoe wouldn't budge. But I could feel its thin hull trembling like the skin of a drum. Something was pummelling it from the other side. It sounded like a high-pressure hose.

Shishkebab! The peke-peke wasn't just underwater,

it was *under the waterfall*! The whole weight of the Matatoro River was crashing down on its upturned hull, pressing it against the rocks. No wonder I couldn't lift it.

I tried freeing my other arm, but it was pinned down like the rest of me. One of the packs sat squarely on my chest, jammed between me and the hull of the peke-peke. I was at the bottom of the pile, with all that weight on top of me, squashed down like one of Uncle Shaun's botanical specimens in a leaf press. I was only alive thanks to a tiny pocket of air trapped in the narrow wedge of floor-space above my mouth and nose. Already the air was growing stale. I was running out of oxygen.

'Gotta get out!' I muttered, straining to wriggle free.

It was useless. The more I struggled, the quicker I was using up the small amount of oxygen I had left. I had to stay calm.

*Think, Sam, think!*

But it's hard to stay calm and think clearly when you're nearly suffocating. The problem was partly lack of oxygen, and partly the weight of Uncle Shaun's pack pressing down on my chest. I knew the pack was his because it was so big and heavy – filled with scientific equipment. It took up so much space that I couldn't expand my lungs more than halfway.

*Hang on a minute!* said a little voice in my head. *If it's Uncle Shaun's pack, then . . .*

I fumbled with my free hand, trying to find the clips that held it closed. But the pack was lying the wrong way – the opening was at the other end. And it was wedged in so tightly that I couldn't get my hand between it and the hull of the peke-peke to reach the clips.

Then I had an idea. Sucking in as much air as would fit inside my constricted lungs, I held it there for a couple of seconds to get maximum effect, then breathed out – and out, *AND OUT!* – until it felt like my chest was going to cave in.

It worked. By fully deflating my lungs, I allowed the pack to drop a couple of centimetres, easing the pressure between it and the shell of the peke-peke above me. Squeezing my fingers into the gap, I wormed my hand down the side of the pack until I felt one of the square plastic clips. But I couldn't get it undone!

By now I was nearly passing out from lack of oxygen. I had to take another gulp of musty air. My chest expanded, squeezing the pack hard against my arm. But I could still move my fingers. Trying not to panic, I fumbled with the clip. Where was the release mechanism? Again I forced all the air out of my lungs. When the pressure eased on my hand, I twisted the clip around and located the release-button with my thumb.

*Click!* I was in.

I'd opened one of the pack's outer compartments, where Uncle Shaun kept his soil sampling tools. At the top was a little sharp-nosed trowel. I dragged it out, turned it around so the blade was pointing down and began frantically digging into the stony riverbed beneath my right hip.

Or *trying* to dig. *Scrape, scrape, scrape.* The rocks were like iron.

After about a minute of useless scratching and scraping, I had to stop for a rest. I was dizzy from lack of oxygen and puffing like a marathon runner. But worse than that, my chest was caving in. I'd completely run out of air!

That was when I remembered something my big brother once told me. Nathan is a tour guide with an outback adventure company in Australia. He's a survival expert and his advice had got me out of tight situations in the past. Here's what he said:

*Keep a cool head, bro.*

Good advice, but difficult to put into practice when you're stuck beneath an upturned boat under a waterfall. Every fibre of your being is on the brink of panic. But if you panic, you're dead.

'Keep a cool head,' I muttered to myself.

And changed my grip on the trowel.

This time, instead of trying to dig into the iron-hard riverbed beneath me, I pushed the trowel's tip sideways into a tiny gap between the edge of the peke-peke and a big stone.

Then, using all the strength left in my body, I levered upwards.

# 4
# DINNER TIME

We'd studied levers at school. Mr Anderson, our science teacher, showed us how you can move something really big (like a peke-peke) if you use something small (like a trowel) as a lever.

Science rocks!

One twist of the trowel, and the peke-peke lifted. Only by a few centimetres, but enough to ease the pressure on everything sandwiched underneath. Including me. Suddenly my other arm was free. So were my legs.

I was right out of oxygen and only a matter of seconds from blacking out, but after my success with the lever, my muscles were pumped up with adrenaline.

That's the body's last line of defence in emergency situations. Adrenaline raises the blood-sugar levels and increases the heart rate, making you faster and stronger. Sometimes it enables you to do things that are almost superhuman. Like lifting a six-metre peke-peke with an outboard motor attached and tossing it to one side.

*Yaaaaaaaaaah!*

Now I could breathe again, but there was another problem. Without the peke-peke above me, I was exposed to the full power of the Big Beast. It hit me with the force of a giant water cannon, slamming me back down against the rocks. Desperately, I heaved Uncle Shaun's pack above my face for protection.

Then, straining to keep the pack in position, I struggled into a sitting position and looked around me. There wasn't much to see. I was sitting chest-deep in the river, surrounded by a brown, liquid curtain where the waterfall came pouring down around the edges of Uncle Shaun's pack. The pack acted like an umbrella, but it weighed a tonne – not just from all of Uncle Shaun's gear, but from the force of the waterfall crashing down on top. I wasn't sure how much longer

I could hold it. But without protection from the Big Beast, I had no hope.

Summoning all my strength, I clambered to my feet in the knee-deep water. It took a huge effort. My legs felt like jelly. Blindly, I took a single, shaky step through the tumbling brown curtain of water.

A rock rolled under my foot. I pitched forward.

*Splash!*

I was underwater again. Face down on the rocky riverbed. Eyes closed, holding my breath. Exhausted. I didn't want to come up. Didn't want to expose myself to another pummelling from the Big Beast. I'd dropped Uncle Shaun's pack when I fell, and I no longer had the strength to lift it again. But I needed air. Gritting my teeth, I raised my head.

Nothing happened. No water came crashing down on my head. Dazed, I took in my surroundings. Slowly, it began to make sense. I was *behind* the waterfall, kneeling in a small hidden lake. About 30 metres long by ten metres wide, it was surrounded on three sides by mossy rock walls. The Big Beast formed the fourth side, a foaming wall of water that cut me off completely from the outside world. A boulder the size of a house formed the ceiling. Thousands of years ago, it must have rolled over the falls and become wedged halfway down, altering the flow of the waterfall and creating an eerie green cavern underneath.

I was probably the first human being ever to be there.

But not the first *living* being.

*Swish-slosh!*

About ten metres away, a circle of ripples radiated out towards the lake's edges. I scrambled quickly to my feet. It was dim in the cavern, but I glimpsed a flash of scales in the dark-green water.

Just a fish, I thought.

Then I remembered where I was. The Amazon. I also remembered the bite marks on the handle of Caesar's knife.

The fish might be a piranha.

My right knee was stinging. I must have grazed it when I fell over on the rocks. A red line of blood trickled down my shin into the water. If there were piranhas in the lake, the blood was a message to them – *come and get me!*

I didn't wait for the piranhas to get their dinner invitation. In five seconds flat, I was out of the lake, crouching on a narrow mossy ledge at the back of the cavern. Safe from the threat of piranhas. But when I shuffled along the ledge looking for a way out, I discovered it stopped after only a few metres. I was trapped. The only way out of the cavern was back through the lake and under the waterfall.

*No way, Jose!*

But I *had* to get out. Uncle Shaun and Caesar would never find me if I stayed where I was.

Thinking about Uncle Shaun drew my eyes to his pack. It lay partially submerged in the lake about eight metres away. Uncle Shaun's boots were inside it. They were made of heavy leather, with high canvas gaiters for leg protection against leeches and prickly vines. They might work against piranhas, too.

But I'd have to wade through the lake to get them.

I looked at my grazed knee. The trickle of blood had made it all the way down to my ankle. It gave me an idea.

Ripping a big wad of moss off the rock wall behind

me, I mopped up the blood. Then I waited a few minutes for more blood to appear and mopped that up, too. After the second time, the graze stopped bleeding. Hoping there was enough blood, I stood up and hurled the soggy lump of moss down the other end of the lake.

'Dinner time!' I yelled as it splashed into the water.

The result was disappointing. Instead of the piranha feeding frenzy I'd expected, the moss sank out of view with hardly a ripple.

So much for my decoy.

Perhaps I was wrong. Perhaps the scales I'd glimpsed belonged to another kind of fish. It might be OK to go back into the lake.

*Swish-slosh!*

Another circle of ripples spread across the lake's dark surface. It was nowhere near the place where the moss had landed. Straining my eyes, I caught a fleeting glimpse of a large underwater shadow that quickly vanished in the soupy green water. Whatever kind of fish it was, it had looked much bigger than a piranha. Could it be a giant Amazonian catfish? Caesar said they grew up to two metres long.

Suddenly I stopped thinking about fish. Something glinted in the rock where I'd torn off the wad of moss. It looked like yellow tinfoil. Or like . . .

Next moment I was down on my hands and knees, tearing off big handfuls of moss to expose what was hidden behind it.

I could hardly believe my eyes.

Holy guacamole! I'd discovered gold!

# 5
# AMBUSH

There was *heaps* of it! The more moss I tore off, the more gold I exposed. A ten-centimetre-wide strip of the precious yellow metal ran right across the shelf and up the rock wall as high as I could reach.

With shaking hands, I cleared away more moss further along the wall and found a second strip of gold. Then another one after that. Wherever I tore away moss, there was gold underneath. My mouth went dry. The entire rear wall of the cavern was a single, enormous gold nugget! It was bigger than a house.

One gram of gold is worth hundreds of dollars. This nugget must have weighed *tonnes*.

I was going be the richest person on earth!

Gold fever does strange things to you. Without giving another thought to piranhas or giant catfish, I waded boldly into the lake and fetched Uncle Shaun's pack.

Most of his equipment was for measuring how global warming is changing the Amazon rainforest. But there was a small tomahawk, too. It had a stainless steel blade. Stainless steel is much harder than gold. Working like a madman, I hacked out three jagged lumps of gold from the wall. The largest one was roughly the size of a Mars Bar and must have weighed about a kilogram. When I hefted it in my hand, I had a sudden reality check.

*How can I carry all this?*

Good question. I didn't even know how I was going to get *myself* out of the cave, much less a stack of gold.

It was time to think about priorities. Top of the list was survival. I was trapped behind a waterfall 300 kilometres up a remote tributary of the Amazon River. It didn't matter that I'd just made the biggest gold discovery of all time; if I couldn't get out and find Uncle Shaun and Caesar, I was history.

There was only one way out – *through* the Big Beast.

I could see a pale glow of daylight on the other side. The wall of water couldn't have been more than two metres thick. That mightn't sound like much, but imagine a line of giant fire hoses, each with a nozzle two metres wide, blasting straight down. No way would I get through without the protection of Uncle Shaun's pack.

I would need his boots and gaiters, too, in case there *were* piranhas. The boots were huge – size twelve – so I wore all three pairs of Uncle Shaun's thick woollen socks. Then I emptied everything else out of his pack and left it on the rock shelf with my sandals.

Lifting the empty pack over my head like an umbrella, I stepped into the lake and started wading towards the waterfall.

Then I stopped.

*Swish-slosh!*

This time the swirl was close. Only a few metres away. A long, scaly shadow came sliding through the water towards me. There were light scales and dark scales, arranged in a diamond pattern that kept repeating itself, over and over, like the windows of a speeding train.

*Shishkebab!*

Suddenly the lake's surface broke open and a big, ugly dinosaur-like head rose out of the water. And it kept rising, up and up and up, until it towered over me.

It was a green anaconda. I'd seen them in wildlife documentaries. They're the biggest snakes in the world. This one didn't look pleased to see me. Or perhaps it *was* pleased. Because a snake that size has an appetite to match.

Of all the giant snakes, the green anaconda is the most dangerous. It does nearly all of its hunting underwater. It will lie just below the surface, a few metres off shore, coiled like a huge underwater spring, waiting for its next meal – a capybara, a deer, a *human* – to come within range.

I'd walked into an anaconda ambush.

Anacondas are constrictors. They wrap themselves around their prey and squeeze until it suffocates. But first they strike like any other snake, and grab hold with their jaws.

The last thing I saw was the inside of the anaconda's wide-open mouth. Coming straight at me.

*WHACK!*

# 6
# BULL KILLER

I was holding Uncle Shaun's pack above my head when the anaconda ambushed me. There was just time to swing it forward in a partial block. Straight into the anaconda's jaws.

*WHACK!*

Uncle Shaun's pack absorbed most of the shock, but not all of it. It felt like I'd run into a brick wall. Or the wall had run into *me*! The snake was huge. As thick as a tree trunk and who knows how long. Pushing and chewing on the pack, it began driving me backwards. One step, two steps, three, four, five. I had to stay on my feet. If I tripped or lost my balance, it would be all over red rover. The anaconda knew it, too. Raising itself out of the water in a series of loops like giant tractor tyres, it corkscrewed sideways, twisting the pack out of my hands. In a last desperate attempt to escape, I threw myself backwards. But my foot slipped and I went under.

I thought I was dead. Water is an anaconda's natural element. In a couple of heartbeats, it would wind me up in its deadly coils and start to squeeze. But nothing happened. I scrambled upright, blinking water from my eyes. The giant snake was nowhere near me. It was halfway across the lake, wrapped around Uncle Shaun's pack in a huge, squirming knot that rolled over and over in the water in an anaconda's version of a death spiral.

Uncle Shaun's pack was the perfect decoy. The snake must have thought it was me – or part of me – and it was so busy trying to crush the life out of it that it didn't notice when I climbed back onto the rock shelf at the rear of the cave.

I was out of the water, but I was far from safe. The ledge was only a metre high. The enormous anaconda wouldn't even have to leave the water to get me. It could simply stretch its head up, grab me by a foot, a leg or an arm, and drag me in.

But I wouldn't make things easy for it. The contents of Uncle Shaun's pack lay strewn across the ledge where I'd dropped them.

My eyes fell on the tomahawk.

But there was something even better: a little crossbow that Uncle Shaun used to shoot down leaves that grew high in the forest canopy. He'd dismantled it to fit in the pack. My hands were trembling, but it only took a minute to fit the curved fibreglass bow to the short, rifle-shaped firing mechanism and tighten the two wing nuts that held it together. I drew back the string and clipped it into the trigger assembly, then fitted an arrow into place. The arrows had bright-orange feathers and wide stainless-steel tips especially designed for cutting though the stems of leaves. They were razor sharp. At close range, they could do a lot of damage to a snake. Even a giant one.

Out in the lake, everything was still. The top of Uncle Shaun's pack, looking as wrecked as a scrunched-up crisp packet, poked out of the water a couple of metres from the Big Beast. But there was no sign of the other big beast – the one that gave the Rio Matatoro its name. On our first day on the river, Caesar told me that *matatoro* was Brazilian for anaconda. It means 'bull killer'. A giant anaconda is big enough, and strong enough, to kill and swallow a bull. Whole! Or so legend has it.

I aimed the crossbow at the water below me.

'Bring it on, Matatoro!' I muttered.

I didn't mean it. It was a warning – I was telling the snake *not* to come after me. I didn't want either of us to get hurt.

But I wasn't going to get my wish.

# 7
# DRACULA

'Ouch!'

I don't know how long I'd been sitting there, aiming the crossbow at the dark-green water, waiting for the anaconda to appear and hoping it wouldn't, when something jabbed me on my right calf. It felt like a needle prick. I took one hand off the crossbow and slapped at my leg, expecting it to be a mosquito or one of the annoying biting flies that are so common in the Amazon. But my hand hit something furry. Something with teeth.

*Ooooooow!*

I jerked my hand away, but the teeth didn't let go. A small greyish-brown animal dangled from my hand.

It looked like a mouse except it had a flat, pig-like nose, large pink ears and long leathery wings. It was a bat. And its teeth were buried in the soft flap of skin between my right thumb and forefinger.

I tried shaking it off, but the evil-looking creature held on. Only when I dropped the crossbow and grabbed the bat with my other hand did it let go. I flung it away from me in revulsion. Towards the lake. A snack for the anaconda. But as it tumbled through the air, the bat unfurled its wings and went flapping away across the water towards the far end of the lake. It circled a couple of times, then flew into a crack in the mossy rock wall and disappeared.

I looked at my hand, at the two bleeding incisions made by the bat's teeth. My leg was bleeding, too – just above the gaiter at the top of my right boot. The bat had crept up and bitten me while my attention was on the water. Neither bite hurt very much, but there was a churning feeling in my stomach as I remembered something I'd read in a travel guide to the Amazon.

In the section entitled *Animal Hazards*. About vampire bats.

I'd read it on the flight from Australia and it had surprised me. I hadn't realised that vampires were real.

They *are* real. And now I'd been bitten by one!

*Swish-slosh!*

I grabbed the crossbow, all thoughts of vampires gone from my head. My mouth felt dry again and my heart pounded as I searched for the anaconda. It wasn't hard to find. A circle of ripples radiated out across the lake. At its centre, a scaly pair of nostrils poked above the surface.

The rest of the reptile was concealed by the soupy green water. I couldn't see its eyes but I could *feel* them watching me. Sizing me up. To a giant anaconda living in a secret lake with just bats and maybe a few fish to snack on, I must have looked like a pretty good meal.

But I had news for the anaconda: I wasn't on the menu. Rising slowly to my feet, I aimed the crossbow just behind the two black pits of its nostrils and curled my finger around the trigger.

*Slosh!*

The nostrils disappeared. There was just an empty circle of ripples in the middle of the lake. Slowly easing the pressure on the trigger, I kept the crossbow pointed at the spot. But the seconds ticked past and there was no sign of the anaconda. I looked at my watch. It was one-thirty in the afternoon. More than half the day was gone already. In a few hours it would start growing dark. The thought of spending the night in the cavern sent a shiver down my spine.

'UNCLE SHAUN!' I yelled. 'CAESAAAAAAR!'

I should have saved my breath. They'd never hear me, even if they were just on the other side of the waterfall. The roar of the Big Beast was too loud.

But bats' ears are better than humans'. My shouting woke up two more vampire bats. They went fluttering silently overhead, doing long loops around the cavern from one end to the other. I kept a nervous eye on them. But it was hard watching the bats and watching the water at the same time. I was glad when they finally disappeared into the crack where the first bat had gone.

'Don't come back,' I muttered, raising one hand to wipe the sweat off my forehead.

Then I froze.

My hand, wrist and forearm were red with blood.

It was dribbling down from the two tiny incisions where the first bat had bitten me.

The bite on my calf was bleeding, too.

A shudder passed through me. Now I remembered what I'd read about vampire bats in the Amazon travel guide. Their saliva contains a substance called draculin that stops the blood from clotting. If you get bitten, you keep bleeding.

And that's not the worst bit. Vampire bats carry rabies, a truly gruesome disease. There's a movie where the family dog gets rabies and turns into a howling, foamy-mouthed killer that infects everything it bites. Nature's version of a zombie.

I needed to sterilise the bites, then stop the bleeding somehow.

There was a first-aid kit among Uncle Shaun's gear. Keeping the crossbow aimed at the water, I knelt on the mossy shelf and used one hand to open the plastic box with the big red cross on its lid. The first thing I saw was an EpiPen. It nearly made me smile. Good old Mum! Uncle Shaun was her younger brother; she must have bullied him into bringing along an extra one for me, just in case. But it wasn't an EpiPen I needed now, it was disinfectant to clean the vampire bat bites, and plasters to stop the bleeding.

I found what I needed and got to work. It was hard patching myself up using only one hand, but no way was I going to put the crossbow down. I knew the anaconda was watching me. A couple of times – when I was opening the antiseptic bottle, for example – it could have got me while I was distracted. But it stayed out of sight. Watching and waiting. Biding its time.

Reptiles are patient. A snake only has to eat once a month. Sooner or later, I would have to sleep. Then the anaconda would make its move.

And so would the vampire bats. There were lots of them in the cave. Now that I knew what they looked like, I could make out a big colony hanging in a dark recess in the rocky ceiling almost directly above me.

I could see their beady black eyes watching me and their little pig-like snouts quivering.

Stay put, bats, I thought, as I stuck the last plaster in place.

Then I had another thought. How did they get in here

in the first place? Unlike the anaconda, bats don't swim. And they were too small and fragile to come through the waterfall like I did. So there must be another entrance.

My eyes darted to the crack in the rock where the three flying bats had disappeared. It looked about 30 centimetres wide – I *might* be able to squeeze through. Provided it didn't get any narrower. And provided it actually led somewhere.

But the crack was right down the far end of the cavern. To reach it, I would have to wade through the water.

*Yeah, right!*

But what choice did I have? I couldn't just stay where I was and wait for the anaconda to make the first move. It might wait three weeks. I'd be dead by then. Either from starvation, rabies, or being sucked dry by the vampire bats.

If I wanted to survive, I had to make the first move.

But first I had to be sure that the crack wasn't a dead end. Using the tomahawk, I chopped the stainless-steel point off one of the arrows. Then I loaded the crossbow, aimed up at the colony of bats dangling from the cave roof, and squeezed the trigger.

*Houston, we have lift-off!*

Bats went everywhere, zooming around the cavern like a mouse-plague with wings. One eye on the bats, I quickly reloaded the crossbow – with a steel-tipped arrow this time – and waited to see what would happen.

Sure enough, after circling a few times, bat after bat disappeared into the crack at the other end of the lake. Soon every last one of them was gone. And not a single bat came back out.

I'd found their secret exit.

But was it big enough for me to go through? And could I even get to it without being taken by the giant anaconda?

There was only one way to find out.

# 8.
# TWANG!

My cargo shorts had four pockets. I filled them with stuff I'd unloaded from Uncle Shaun's pack. The canoe and all our supplies were gone, so the more I took with me, the better my chances (and Uncle Shaun's and Caesar's chances – provided I found them soon) of making it back to civilisation alive.

Most of what I took came from the first-aid kit: the EpiPen, some plasters and adhesive dressings in a sealed plastic bag, the bottle of antiseptic, and Uncle Shaun's anti-malaria pills. I also took the little folding scalpel that my uncle used to dissect leaves and plant specimens.

Last of all, I squeezed in one of the lumps of gold. It was heavy and tugged at the waistband of my shorts, but if I didn't have evidence, nobody would take me seriously when I said I wanted to come back to the Amazon and start a gold mine.

But first I had to get *out* of the Amazon. Which meant getting out of the cavern. And that meant – my skin prickled at the thought – going back into the lake where the giant anaconda was lurking.

With the loaded crossbow in one hand and the two remaining arrows in the other, I stepped down into the knee-deep water. It was the worst feeling. I had no idea where the snake was, but I did know one thing: it knew where *I* was.

Swinging the crossbow back and forth, I started wading around the edge of the lake. I stayed as close to the wall as I could. It protected my left flank, narrowing the anaconda's options.

Halfway to my destination, I began to get a really strong feeling that the anaconda was behind me. In my mind's eye, I saw it weaving along the bottom of the lake, invisible in the dark water as it stealthily closed in on my heels. Hair standing on end, I slowly turned around.

It was lucky I did. Because suddenly the lake's surface burst open and a huge, pink mouth exploded out of the water.

There was just enough time to swing the crossbow around and release an arrow.

*Twang!*

# 9
# DEAD END

All hell broke loose. The anaconda rolled into a knot the size of a hatchback car and began turning over and over like a water turbine. It sent clouds of spray as high as the rocky ceiling. It sent foaming waves right across the lake to the waterfall on the other side. It drenched me with flying water.

I backed away for a couple of metres, then turned and waded flat out the rest of the way to the crack in the wall. It *did* look like the mouth of tunnel, and it *was* wide enough for me to squeeze through. But I hesitated. It was completely dark inside. What if it was just the entrance to another underground chamber, and the vampire bats were all crowded inside, waiting for me to come and join them? I wished I had a torch. There was one back on the ledge with the rest of Uncle Shaun's things, but it was too big to fit in my pockets so I hadn't brought it with me. Bad decision. I glanced over my shoulder.

The anaconda was gone.

It's probably dead, I thought. Maybe my arrow had hit it in the throat. It was safe to go back for the torch.

I turned to retrace my steps, but something caught my eye. Orange feathers. A crossbow arrow was embedded in the moss a few metres past where I'd last seen the anaconda. It must have glanced off the reptile's leathery scales and ricocheted into the wall.

So the anaconda *wasn't* dead. I'd only nicked it. Hurt it enough to make it lose its cool, but not enough to kill it.

Then I saw something that made me freeze. Ripples. Not ripples that moved out in concentric circles, but ripples that moved in lines. Lines that joined in a V. And the point of the V was moving. Straight towards me.

*Get out of the lake!* screamed the little voice inside my head.

I did fit into the tunnel. Just. It was a tight squeeze. I pushed the crossbow and arrows in ahead of me, then hauled myself out of the water and wriggled in after them.

The tunnel sloped upwards. It was a good sign. When you're underground and want to get out, up is the best direction. But I could see nothing ahead of me. No sign of daylight. No sign of *anything*. I needed Uncle Shaun's torch. Praying that the tunnel really was an escape route, I wormed my way blindly through the inky darkness. Despite all the evidence that told me I was climbing, in my imagination it felt like I was going *down*, burrowing steadily towards the centre of the earth. Towards my doom.

I started to regret filling my pockets. It made me really fat around my thighs. It was slowing me down. None of the first-aid gear (or the gold) would be any good to me if I got stuck.

Or if something worse happened.

I could hear a dry scuffling noise behind me, like scales sliding across rock. Holy guacamole, the anaconda was coming after me!

I couldn't use the crossbow. There wasn't room to twist around and shoot my two arrows back down the tunnel. My only chance was to keep going. To try to outrun the anaconda. Or out*wriggle* it, because wriggling along on my belly was the only way to move through the increasingly narrow tunnel. But snakes have it over humans when it comes to wriggling.

One thing gave me hope. The anaconda was huge. Not just long, but fat. It was bigger around the middle than me. Maybe it couldn't fit all the way up the tunnel. It might get stuck.

There was a danger I might get stuck, too. A very real danger. The tunnel was getting smaller. I reached a point where the ceiling came down so low, I had to turn my head sideways to fit through. There was barely room for my body to follow. It felt like I was wriggling into a grave. But anything was better than being eaten by a giant anaconda. I could still hear a faint scuffling noise behind me. Blindly I pushed forward, feeling my way ahead with the crossbow.

*Clunk!*

It hit rock. I'd reached a dead end. I was trapped.

'*HELP!*' I yelled, finally giving way to panic. '*UNCLE SHAUN! CAESAR! HELP!*'

There was no echo this time. Just a fluttering sound and a tiny movement of air that tickled the hairs of my right forearm.

Vampire bat! I thought, and lashed out blindly with the crossbow.

*Crack!* My arm smacked into the tunnel wall, right on the funny bone. *Ooooow!* I dropped the crossbow and clutched my tingling elbow.

*Bang . . . clatter . . . slide . . . scrape!*

What was that? I froze and listened, but the noises had stopped. They had come from just in front of me, where I'd dropped the crossbow. I reached forward into the darkness, but nothing was there. *Literally* nothing. My hand dangled in empty space.

There was a hole in the floor right in front of me. A hole big enough for the crossbow to fall through.

It wasn't a dead end!

I wormed forward and found myself looking down a narrow rocky chute. Yes, *looking*! A wash of pale light gleamed up from below. I couldn't see where it was coming from because two metres below me the chute curved out of sight like a water slide. It was wet like a water slide, too. Water seeped out of a crack in the wall near my shoulder and trickled down the chute, making it green with slime. It looked slippery.

I dropped the two arrows, one at a time, and watched them zip down the chute and disappear around the curve.

Hooley dooley! I thought, chewing my lower lip and trying to build up my courage.

I had no idea what was at the bottom, nor how steep it was around the curve, nor whether the natural water slide would stay wide enough all the way down. But there was one way to find out.

I wriggled out over the rocky lip of the chute. There wasn't room to turn around and go down feet first. I took a deep breath, then launched myself headlong into the abyss.

# 10
# TWO MINUTES
# TO LIVE

I must have closed my eyes. Because I have no visual memories of what happened next. Just a sensation of speed. And of a wet, super-slippery surface swishing past underneath me.

Then – for about half a second – *nothing* was underneath me.

*SPLOSH!*

I opened my eyes and saw sky. I was out.

Out of the cave that is, but not out of trouble. My legs and lower body felt strange – sort of cool and wet and . . . *stuck*! I'd landed in a mud hole. It was about three metres across and surrounded by reeds. Looming overhead, a tall rocky escarpment blocked out half the sky. Partway up the craggy cliff face was a small round hole with water trickling out of it. That's where I'd come from. I would have been seriously injured if not for my muddy splash-down.

But now I wanted to get out and I was having trouble. The mud was really thick. It was hard to move my legs. When I tried to make for the nearest reeds – half-wading, half-swimming – I wasn't getting anywhere. The only direction I was going was *down*.

Shishkebab! I'd landed in quicksand!

I could hardly believe my bad luck. I'd survived so much – fire ants, the peke-peke's propeller, the Big Beast, vampire bats, claustrophobia, near suffocation, and being ambushed by the BIGGEST SNAKE IN THE WORLD – yet I was *still* going to die. I would never see my family again. Never get to tell anyone about the gold I'd discovered. Never be a millionaire.

But I wasn't dead yet. And I was back in the outside world, no longer trapped in a cave.

'HEEEEEEEEEELP!' I yelled at the absolute top of my voice. 'UNCLE SHAUN! CAESAR!'

This time they might be able to hear me. But they would have to be really close, because the roar of the Big Beast was even louder out here than it had been in the cave. I couldn't see the waterfall because the reeds blocked my view, but I could see a fine mist of spray coming around the edge of the rocky escarpment.

*Hang on a minute!* said the little voice in my head. *Shouldn't the waterfall be in the* other *direction?*

I thought about being swept over the Big Beast, and made a map in my head of the secret lake and the ledge and the position of the tunnel. Suddenly it made sense – I'd crossed behind the waterfall and come out on the other side of the river!

Even if Uncle Shaun and Caesar *did* hear me, they wouldn't be able to come to my rescue.

I was on my own. Stuck in quicksand. And sinking. The more I struggled, the faster I went down. The bubbling brown mud was up to my rib cage. I couldn't reach the reeds. I searched desperately for something – *anything!* – to grab onto. That was when I noticed a small, muddy prong poking out of the quicksand to my right. It was the tip of the crossbow.

I dragged it out of the mud, hooked it around five or six of the nearest reeds and started pulling them towards me. They bent like giant grass stalks. I grabbed them with my free hand and dropped the crossbow. Bunching them in both hands, I tried to pull myself out of the quicksand.

*Slurp!*

The reeds came out by the roots. Shishkebab! I was going to die!

*Keep a cool head,* I remembered.

But it was easier said than done. I was sinking. Slowly and steadily, the quicksand was dragging me down. It already reached my armpits. In another two minutes, it would be up to my head.

I had two minutes to live. All I could do was call for help – *'UNCLE SHAUN! CAESAR!'* – even though I knew it was hopeless.

The quicksand closed around my neck like cold, sticky porridge.

*'HEEEEEEEELP!'*

There was a rustling sound, then the *slop, slop, slop* of feet walking in mud.

I twisted my head around. An Indian stood at the edge of the reeds. He wasn't dressed in European clothes like the Indians further down the river. All he wore was a kind of loincloth made of woven fibre, and two red feathers that dangled from his earlobes. His straight black hair was cut flat around the bottom like a helmet. In one hand he held a long, skinny blowgun. In the other, he clutched a black-tipped poison dart.

'Can you help me out of here?' I said.

The Indian scowled and said something in the strange, whispery language of the Yanomami people we'd met on our way upriver.

Then he pointed the blowgun straight at my head.

# 11
# THOUSANDS
# OF TEETH

'He say to take hold,' a voice said in English.

A second Indian had appeared from behind the reeds, a boy of about seven or eight. He wasn't wearing *anything*. Just a smile.

'Father pull you out,' he said.

Hoping there wasn't a poison dart in the blowgun, I grabbed hold with both hands and the boy's father slowly hauled me up onto the mat of spongy reeds where the two Indians were standing. I lost one of Uncle Shaun's boots in the gluey quicksand, but the boy fished it out with a stick. After tipping the mud out of it, I pulled it back on.

'Thank you.'

'You welcome,' the boy said shyly.

I must have looked terrible – plastered from head to toe in sticky brown gloop. Using a clump of reeds, I wiped the mud off my face and arms. The man watched me with narrowed eyes.

'Garimpeiro?' he grunted. It didn't sound like the soft Yanomami language he'd been speaking before, it sounded like a swear word.

'He say are you prospector?' the boy translated.

I nervously touched the heavy lump of gold in my pocket. The tone of the question – and the way both Indians frowned as they waited for my reply – told me that they didn't like prospectors. I shook my head. 'I'm here with my uncle. He's a scientist who studies trees.'

Again there were frowns. 'For cut them down?' the boy asked.

'No, my uncle loves trees,' I said quickly. 'He wants to stop people cutting them down.'

The man nodded when his son translated. As if he loved trees, too.

'Where is uncle?'

'On the other side of the river. We got separated and I was swept over the waterfall.'

When the man heard this, he looked impressed. He spoke rapidly to his son.

'Father say you welcome in our forest. Big Beast give you respect.'

I decided not to say anything about what had happened *after* I was swept over the waterfall. I didn't want them to know about the secret cave, and I especially didn't want them to know about the gold.

The man used his blowgun to lift the crossbow out of the quicksand. The boy found both arrows in the reeds around the other side. They had never seen a crossbow before so I showed them how it worked. I used a reed stalk instead of an arrow because there were only two left. The man asked if he could have a turn, but he wanted a real arrow, not a reed stalk. He'd just saved my life, so I couldn't refuse. He aimed the crossbow up at the escarpment. Only then did I see a small, rat-like animal crouched on a rocky ledge about five metres from the top. *Twang!* The arrow missed by miles and disappeared over the escarpment. Grinning, the Indian handed the crossbow back. Then he offered me his blowgun and pointed at the rat. I shook my head – I didn't want to shoot the rat or waste one of his poison darts.

'Can you help me find my uncle?' I asked.

The boy relayed the question to his father, who shook his head.

'Father say first we take monkey to village,' the boy translated.

Before I could ask, 'What monkey?' the Indians disappeared through the reeds into the jungle. I followed them to a small clearing, where a howler monkey lay stone dead on a log. They must have been returning from a hunting expedition when they heard my cries for help.

Next to the dead monkey lay a wooden quiver of poison darts and a water gourd.

'Can I have a drink?' I asked.

'Certain,' said the boy.

The water tasted muddy but I didn't care – it was the first drink I'd had since just before Uncle Shaun spotted the sloth. I could have emptied the gourd five times over, but I remembered to leave some for the boy and his father.

'My name's Sam,' I said, tapping my chest so the man would understand.

'I am Gabriel,' said the boy.

I had expected something more unusual – an Indian name. 'What's your father called?' I asked.

'Father not have school name.'

'What's his Yanomami name?'

The boy shook his head. 'I not allowed to say for you.'

I wanted to ask why, but now wasn't the time. 'Is it far to the village, Gabriel?'

'Not far,' he said.

I had to look the other way when his father lifted the monkey carcass across his shoulders. I'd seen dead animals before, but never a monkey. It put a lump in my throat.

'Why do you hunt monkeys?' I whispered to Gabriel as his father led us along a narrow path that went deep into the jungle.

'For eat,' he said, patting his stomach. 'You are hungry?'

I shook my head. I *was* hungry, but no way in the world was I going to eat monkey. I hoped there would be other food at the village. Gabriel reckoned it wasn't far.

Half an hour later, I began to wonder about his understanding of English. How far was *not far*? We must have walked several kilometres through the jungle. Worse, we seemed to be travelling away from the river. Which meant we were moving away from Uncle Shaun and Caesar.

I tapped Gabriel's shoulder. 'I'm going back.'

He shook his head. 'You come to village.'

'It's too far.'

'Not far,' he said.

I stopped in the middle of the track. Half an hour ago he'd said the same thing. 'I'm going back,' I said. 'I have to find my uncle.'

'Uncle be OK.'

'He'll be worried sick. If he and Caesar don't find me before dark, they might start back down the river without me.'

Gabriel's father came back to see why we'd stopped. A cloud of flies buzzed around the dead monkey. He spoke rapidly to his son, waving the blowgun at the vine-entangled trees that pressed in on both sides of the track.

'Father say jaguar eat you.'

I knew about jaguars. As savage as leopards and as big as lions, they are the top predator on the Amazon food chain.

'I can look after myself,' I said, my hands sweaty on the loaded crossbow. 'Thank your father for me, Gabriel. And thank you, too. I really appreciate all your help. But I've got to go back and find my uncle.'

Turning, I began walking back down the track the way we'd come. But I didn't get far – only ten or 12 paces. Then I stopped dead.

What was that rumbling sound?

The others heard it, too.

'Climb tree!' called Gabriel.

I looked over my shoulder. Already he was two metres off the ground, shinnying up a liana vine. His father had left the dead monkey in the fork of a sapling and threaded the blowgun through the waistband of his loincloth. With the darts quiver swinging from his back, he scrambled up a big, smooth-trunked tree that had shiny leaves shaped like elephants' ears.

The rumbling noise grew louder, and a flock of huge

red-and-blue parrots – scarlet macaws – went flying overhead, shrieking in alarm. They were followed by a giant-billed toucan. Then a little scaly armadillo came scuttling out of the undergrowth. It raced past me as if I wasn't even there, fleeing from the rumbling sound.

*'CLIMB TREE!'* Gabriel yelled.

None of the trees near me looked easy to climb – and I couldn't shinny up a vine wearing Uncle Shaun's boots – so I started running towards the elephant-ear tree.

*'OTHER WAY!'* yelled Gabriel.

I skidded to a halt.

Something was coming. A wave of swaying vines, jiggling palms and shaking bushes swept towards me through the undergrowth. It looked like a wide, green avalanche. It even rumbled like an avalanche. There was another sound, too – a strange, clicking-grinding sound. Like thousands of teeth.

*'RUN!'* screamed Gabriel.

But it was too late to run. The green avalanche swept past the elephant-ear tree and came rushing towards me.

Bracing myself for the worst, I raised the crossbow.

# 12
# SHISHKEBAB!

The first one came so fast that there wasn't time to pull the trigger.

It burst out of the undergrowth and shot past me almost before I saw it.

But what I did see was enough. A pair of curved yellow tusks, two beady black eyes and a long, low, barrel-shaped body. It was a peccary – a South American relative of the wild pig. And it wasn't alone. The thunder was the sound of galloping hooves. The clicking was the sound of grinding tusks. It was a herd of peccaries on the run. A stampede!

And I was right in their path.

The second peccary broke cover three metres away and came straight for me. There were animals on either side of it and more behind, so it couldn't slow down or swerve to miss me, even if it tried. It didn't try. It lowered its head and charged.

*WHAM!*

It knocked me for six. I landed flat on my back with the peccary on top. We stayed like that, neither of us moving, as the rest of the herd stampeded past on both sides.

Only when they'd gone, and the rumble of their galloping hooves faded into the distance, did I push the peccary off me and sit up. The arrow that I'd shot when the peccary charged was buried all the way to the feathers in the dead animal's neck.

'Sam, stay still!' Gabriel called down softly from his refuge high in the jungle canopy.

I craned my neck to look for him, but saw his father instead. He was still in the elephant-ear tree, supporting himself with one hand and holding the blowgun in the other.

For the second time that day, it was pointing right at me.

'Hey, what's . . . ?'

A deep, throaty growl made the words die in my throat.

Slowly I turned my head.

Shishkebab!

I was looking directly into the honey-coloured eyes of a puma.

# 13
# ANACONDAS DON'T HAVE FINS

I didn't know there were pumas in the Amazon. I thought they were only found in North America. Was I dreaming?

I *hoped* I was dreaming.

The puma bared its eight-centimetre fangs and let out another growl. Warm droplets of spit sprayed my face. No dream could be that real. Nor that terrifying. The big, straw-coloured cat was so close I could have reached across the dead peccary and touched it. But no way in the world was I going to do that – I wanted to keep all my fingers.

I slipped my hand into the top pocket of my shorts, searching for Uncle Shaun's folding scalpel. All I found was a big lump of gold. Wrong pocket.

The puma hissed.

*Steady, boy!*

I tried another pocket. EpiPen, anti-malaria pills – no scalpel.

The puma edged closer until it was standing right over the peccary. Nothing was between us now.

Up in the tree, Gabriel's father spoke softly to his son.

Why doesn't he use the blowgun? I thought. Swivelling my eyes, I saw the problem. I was right in the line of fire. If the poison dart missed the puma, I'd be the one to cop it.

'Father say go back plenty slow,' Gabriel called down to me.

I started inching backwards, crab-like, along the ground. The puma bared its teeth and let out another hiss. But it didn't come after me. All it wanted was the peccary.

When I was three or four metres clear, I rose slowly to my feet and starting backing towards the elephant-ear tree. The puma watched me every step of the way. It had the most ferocious glare – a look that said, *You killed the peccary, but now it's mine.* I wasn't going to argue.

When I reached the tree, I switched from slow motion to fast forward. I went up it like a monkey, and didn't stop until I was higher than Gabriel's father. He was still watching the puma, but he no longer held the blowgun to his lips. Now that I was safe, I was glad he hadn't fired a poison dart at it. A peccary and a monkey were enough dead animals for one day.

Gabriel's father and I stayed in our tree until the puma dragged the peccary into the undergrowth. Then we climbed cautiously back down to the ground. Gabriel came swinging down on a vine like Tarzan.

'Good shooting, Sam,' he said, prodding the remains of the crossbow with his foot. It had been trampled to bits in the stampede. 'You find uncle now?'

I glanced nervously at the spot where the puma had disappeared. 'How far is the village?'

Gabriel grinned and said, 'Not far.'

His father wasn't grinning. His expression was more like a grimace. And he was holding his nose. He said something to Gabriel.

'Father say you wash before go to village,' the boy said. 'Peccary make you smell bad.'

Now that they'd mentioned it, I noticed the bad smell, too. Gross! I've never smelled a skunk, but I reckon they can't be much worse than peccaries. And now the peccary smell was all over me.

Gabriel's father led us to a narrow animal trail that zigzagged downhill to a small creek. There was a pool where a fallen tree had created a dam. The surface was covered in giant water lilies. I couldn't see what was under the huge lily pads, but I didn't care. I was hot, I was caked with dried mud, I *stank*. I ploughed straight in, clothes and all.

I grew up in northern Australia, where you have to be careful if you go swimming. There are crocodiles, leeches and snakes. This was the Amazon jungle. It's even more hazardous for swimmers than northern Australia. There are caimans, piranhas, giant anacondas, parasite fish and freshwater stingrays. And there's something worse – something more dangerous than all the others put together.

At first touch I thought it was just the thick rubbery stem of a water lily dragging across my leg as I waded into the waist-deep water.

But when I stopped, the stem kept moving.

It slid smoothly around my calf like the cold tentacle of an octopus. A very big octopus. But there aren't any octopuses in the Amazon jungle.

Another anaconda! I thought, and froze in terror.

It's lucky I froze. Because when I looked down through a gap between two lily pads, I saw a large bullet-shaped head and two fan-shaped fins. Anacondas don't have fins, fish have fins.

And so do eels.

Holy guacamole! Wrapped around my leg was an electric eel!

# 14
# KILLER KING

The jaguar is the top predator in the Amazon – but only on land. In the water, the electric eel is the undisputed killer king. When it's hunting or feeling threatened, it can produce 600 volts of electricity – enough to kill a horse. It doesn't even have to touch you to be dangerous. Electricity travels through water. You can be swimming five or six metres from an electric eel and still be electrocuted.

And I had one wrapped around my leg. If I moved, or if it saw me as prey, I'd get zapped.

'Sam, what is wrong?' Gabriel asked from the shore.

'There's an electric eel,' I said softly.

Gabriel and his father had a short conversation.

'Father say come out from water plenty plenty slow.'

'It's coiled around my leg.'

Gabriel spoke to his father again. The man muttered something in reply, dropped his blowgun and the dead monkey on the ground, and vanished into the jungle.

'Father get sleepy berry,' Gabriel explained.

Before I could ask what a sleepy berry was, his father returned with a leafy branch. At its tip was a bunch of purple berries. He twisted the bunch free and tossed the berries onto the lily pad next to me.

'Father say squeeze berry, make juice go in water,' Gabriel instructed.

The berries were ripe and soft, full of dark juice that dribbled through my fingers when I squeezed. It created a pink underwater cloud that spread slowly around me until I could no longer see the eel. But I could still feel it wrapped around my leg like a big, soft rope. I hoped the juice of the sleepy berry wouldn't upset it. My survival depended on the eel remaining calm. If it got scared or confused by the pink cloud in the water, it might turn the power on. The big, soft rope would become a high-voltage electricity cable. *ZAP!*

It didn't happen. After about a minute, I felt the creature's grip on my leg begin to relax. Then it let go. I held my breath as the two-metre eel floated to the surface next to my elbow. It wasn't moving.

'Is it dead?' I asked.

'Just sleeping,' said Gabriel. 'Father say you can wash now.'

Within minutes of rejoining the main track, I heard the sound of children's voices ahead. We turned a corner and found ourselves at the edge of a wide jungle clearing. Standing in the middle was an enormous round building made of sticks and logs and palm fronds. It looked big enough to house 50 people. There were gardens all around it. Two women picked long, bean-like vegetables from a row of leafy plants propped up with sticks. A couple of small naked children played nearby. They noticed us and came running. Twenty metres away they stopped and stood gawking at me. We stopped, too. Gabriel's father said something, then walked ahead carrying the monkey. I started to follow, but Gabriel clutched my elbow.

'Father say you wait here.'

I began to feel uneasy. The women had stopped work. One came hurrying forward. She picked up the smaller child, grabbed the other by the hand and hurried away, glancing over her shoulder a couple of times as if she was scared of me. It felt weird. Did she think I was the bogey man?

An old man emerged from the building carrying a stick. He nearly dropped it when he saw me. Another man came out and they both stood staring at me. Gabriel's father walked up to them and started talking. More men joined them. Everyone seemed to talk at once. The old man waved his stick in my direction.

'What are they saying?' I asked Gabriel.

'Some Yanomami not like white man. They say you steal our land and cut down our trees.'

'I wouldn't do that,' I said. 'My uncle came to *save* the trees.'

Gabriel nodded. 'Certain. Father will tell them.'

But nobody was listening to Gabriel's father. More men had come out of the building. Soon he was surrounded by a big noisy mob. Everyone sounded angry. Every so often, someone would point at me and raise his voice. I could guess what they were saying: *Get out of our village!*

'I think I'd better go,' I said softly.

This time Gabriel didn't argue. He was listening to the men and chewing his lower lip. 'You go that way not far,' he said, pointing back down the track. 'Wait for me to come. I will bring for you water and food.'

'Not monkey,' I said.

Gabriel grinned. 'Not monkey.'

I turned and walked back into the jungle. Several of the men started shouting at my back. I didn't blame them for being angry. Other white men – men who looked like me – had done bad things to them and their people in the past. But it was horrible being yelled at and sent away just because of the colour of my skin. I felt like the worst person in the world.

It was a relief to reach the bend in the track where the jungle hid me from their view.

And an even bigger relief to meet someone coming the other way.

'Dr Livingstone, I presume?' he said.

# 15
# THE BRIBE

It was the last thing I expected. We were hundreds of kilometres from the nearest town, in one of the remotest parts of the Amazon, yet here was another white man. *Two* white men – a second one came trudging up the track behind him. Both wore sweat-stained khaki shirts, blue jeans and sneakers that looked brand new. Both were bent under the weight of enormous backpacks. And both carried pistols, strapped to their right hips in brown leather holsters.

'I'm Sam Fox from Australia,' I said, shaking the first man's hand. 'It's good to meet you.'

'Good to meet you, too, Sam Fox from Australia,'

he said. He was short and muscular, with ginger hair and a floppy red moustache. 'I'm Henry and this is Bernard.'

Bernard was tall, with blond hair and shifty blue eyes. He spoke with a strong accent. 'Vot are you doing here, Sam?'

'Looking for my uncle – Dr Shaun Carrington, the famous botanist. He's doing a study of climate change and its effects on the Amazon rainforest. We got separated when some fire ants fell into our canoe and he and our boatman jumped overboard.'

'That explains it then,' said Henry.

'What are *you* doing here?' I asked.

'Following you,' said Bernard, studying my boots. ''Ve came upon your tracks a vile ago and decided to find out vot you are up to.'

'But why are you in the Amazon jungle?'

The two men exchanged a quick glance.

'Looking for rare butterflies,' Henry said. 'We're butterfly collectors.'

They didn't look like butterfly collectors. Where were their nets? And why the big pistols?

'Zere ver other footprints vith yours,' Bernard said,

interrupting my thoughts. 'Bare feet.'

'And we thought we heard shouting,' Henry added.

'Yanomami Indians,' I said. 'A boy and his father. They took me to their village.'

'Vere is zis village?' asked Bernard.

I pointed up the track. 'It's just around the next corner. But they're not very friendly. I think they thought I was a prospector.'

Henry raised his eyebrows. 'Want to know something funny, Sam? When we first found your footprints, we thought you were a prospector, too!'

Both men laughed, and so did I. But I wasn't laughing inside. Because technically I *was* a prospector, and there was a big lump of gold in my pocket to prove it.

'Let's pay your friends a little visit,' said Bernard, hitching his huge pack a little higher on his back as he started to move past me.

'I don't think you should,' I said.

He turned on me, his eyes like chips of ice. 'Ve are not asking your permission, kid,' he snapped. 'Vot ve do is no business of yours.'

Henry patted me on the shoulder. 'Go back and find

your famous uncle. I'm sure he's worried about you.'

'But it's a long way back to the river. What if I meet a jaguar?'

'Chances of that are fairly slim,' he said. 'Jaguars are as rare as hen's teeth and generally they keep away from humans.'

I could hardly believe my ears. He and Bernard seemed like educated men, yet they were leaving me to fend for myself in the Amazon jungle.

'You aren't really butterfly collectors, are you?' I said.

Before Henry or Bernard could answer, a small brown figure came running around the corner from the direction of the village. It was Gabriel. He had put on a pair of baggy shorts and carried a water gourd and a woven basket. He came skidding to a stop when he saw the three of us blocking the track.

'Hello there!' Henry said loudly. 'Do you speak English?'

Gabriel shifted nervously from one bare foot to the other. 'Are you Sam's uncle?'

'No, I'm his friend.'

'They aren't my friends,' I butted in. 'Don't listen to him.'

Henry's elbow dug me in the ribs. 'Shut your mouth!' he hissed. To Gabriel, he said, 'Look, sonny, I've got something for you.'

From a side pocket of his pack, he withdrew a small hand-held computer game. It was bright yellow, about the size of a mobile phone, and when Henry flicked a switch it came to life with a jingling electronic tune.

'Would you like this?' he asked, holding it up for Gabriel to see.

The boy nodded.

I should have said something. Should have told Gabriel that the game's cheap batteries would be dead after he'd played it for a few hours. Should have said that it wasn't a gift, it was a bribe – Henry wanted something from Gabriel in return for the game. But the look in the boy's big brown eyes told me I'd be wasting my time. He lived in an isolated village where they didn't have electricity or TVs or even running water, so a hand-held computer game would seem like something from an eight-year-old's wildest dream.

Dropping the water gourd and basket in the middle of the track, Gabriel came shyly forward. Henry placed the 21st-century toy in his small, outstretched hand.

'It's yours to keep, sonny. Want me to show you how it works?'

While Henry taught Gabriel how to play the computer game, Bernard opened his own pack and pulled out an array of items. There was a plastic doll, a cheap glass necklace, half a dozen Chupa Chups and a pair of red-framed sunglasses. He placed everything on a square of bright cloth in the middle of the track.

'Vot is your name, little boy?' he asked, smiling like a car salesman in a TV ad.

'Gabriel.'

'Gabriel, do you think your parents and family vould like zese qifts?'

The boy nodded.

'Very good.' Bernard gathered the cloth by its four corners, bundling everything inside, and handed it to Gabriel. 'Go to your village and give zese nice gifts to your family. Tell anyone who vants more good things to come here where ve are vaiting.'

Gabriel's smile stretched from ear to ear. It must have seemed like winning a lottery. Clutching the computer game in one hand and the bundle of goodies in the other, he went scampering away.

'The Indians don't need your gifts,' I said to Bernard and Henry. 'They've got everything they need right here in the jungle.'

Bernard turned to me. 'You are still here, troublemaker? Go back to your uncle now, or ve might get rough on you.'

And he tapped the butt of his pistol to show that he meant it.

# 16
# GARIMPEIRO!

Taking the water gourd and the basket that Gabriel had brought for me, I left the two white men and headed down the track. But only until I was out of sight. It was a long way to the river and I was scared of getting lost. But more scared of meeting the puma again, or a jaguar, or another peccary stampede. All I had to protect myself was Uncle Shaun's folding scalpel. Its blade was only two centimetres long. Ducking into the green tangle of vegetation beside the track, I doubled back until I had a clear view of Henry and Bernard through a tiny gap in the undergrowth. Even though I didn't like them – and they didn't like me – it felt safer to be near other humans.

I had a vague plan of following them after they'd finished their business with Gabriel's people, waiting until they'd set up camp, then stealing one of their pistols after they fell asleep. With a pistol I could defend myself against jaguars and pumas, and I could fire shots into the air to attract Uncle Shaun's attention when I reached the river.

I sat down on a mossy log and spied on Henry and Bernard. While I waited for something to happen, I drank half the water from the gourd Gabriel had brought for me, then looked in the basket to see what food he'd packed. There was a big tapioca-bread pancake, two cooked plantains (like little green bananas) wrapped in a big floppy leaf, and a black potato-like vegetable that was burnt on the outside but tasted like boiled egg. Yum! I was so hungry I ate everything.

There was still no sign of the Indians, so I took the opportunity to check out the vampire bat bites on my hand and leg. The bleeding had stopped and both wounds looked clean. But just to be on the safe side I gave them another wash with the disinfectant from my pocket before putting on fresh dressings. I was covered in mosquito bites, so I swallowed an anti-malaria pill and quickly returned everything to my pockets, except the scalpel.

There were voices approaching. About 20 Yanomami men came walking in single file down the track from the village. First in line was the old man who'd waved his stick at me. He wore the red-framed sunglasses and carried his stick. It looked different up close – more like a ceremonial club. Nearly a metre long, it had a bunch of red-and-yellow feathers on one end, and a rock the size of a lemon attached to the other end with twine. Gabriel's father came next, wearing the glass necklace and sucking a Chupa Chup. Several other men were sucking Chupa Chups, too. I spotted Gabriel right at the back, so engrossed in his computer game that he was barely looking where he was going.

The Indians stopped a few metres from Henry and Bernard.

'Greetings, my friends,' Henry said loudly.

None of the Indians said a thing. They didn't understand English.

Henry spotted Gabriel and called him to the front of the group. 'Tell them what I'm saying, kid,' he said. 'They can have one gift each.'

While Gabriel translated, Bernard began lifting more cheap gifts from his pack and holding them up so the Indians could see. There was glass jewellery, a New York Knicks baseball cap, a set of gel pens and a blue plastic watch. The old man pointed his stick at the watch and spoke to Gabriel.

'He want that thing,' the boy said.

Henry shook his head. 'Only one gift each. Grandad already has the sunglasses. But tell him he can have the watch, too, if he brings something for me.'

Gabriel and the old man had a short conversation in Yanomami.

'He say what thing you want?' Gabriel asked.

Henry nodded to Bernard, who unzipped one of the pack's inner pockets and lifted out a small drawstring bag. He tossed it to Henry, who loosened the top and tipped half a dozen small pebbles into his hand. One of the pebbles was speckled with flecks of gold, another flashed red like a ruby.

'Any man who can bring us rocks like these,' Henry said, holding up one of the glistening pebbles, 'can have many gifts.'

All at once it became clear to me what Henry and Bernard were doing in that remote corner of the Amazon jungle. They had come to trade their trashy 'gifts' with the Indians in exchange for gold and jewels.

They were prospectors.

The old man must have worked it out, too. Pointing the ceremonial club at Bernard's chest, he began speaking really fast – too fast for Gabriel to translate. But there was one word I understood – *garimpeiro* – and the old man repeated it several times.

Henry spoke to Bernard out of the side of his mouth. 'Give Grandad the watch before he blows a gasket.'

Bernard held out the watch, but the old man waved it away. He whipped off the red-framed sunglasses and threw them on the ground at Bernard's feet. He was still talking flat out.

'You must go from our land,' Gabriel translated.

'Tell him we have travelled from far away to bring him these gifts,' said Henry.

'He say *garimpeiro* bring bad luck to our people. Many white men will follow your footsteps. They will chop down trees and build roads and dig holes in the earth. They will destroy our home.'

Bernard leaned sideways and spoke softy to Henry. I couldn't hear what he said, but I saw Henry's eyes suddenly fix on the rock tied to the end of the old man's club. Without realising it, the Indian had stepped into a narrow shaft of sunlight that filtered down through the trees. And a transformation had occurred. The rock was dazzling! Lit up from inside, it shot out a thousand beams of rainbow light like a miniature laser show.

There's only one stone that can sparkle like that – a diamond.

Henry wet his lips. 'Tell the old man,' he said to Gabriel, 'that if he gives us one thing, we will give him *all* our gifts. Then we will go away and never come back.'

'What thing?' Gabriel asked.

'His stick.'

'He will not give that,' said Gabriel, solemnly shaking his head. 'It belonged to his father, and to his father before him, and every father come before.'

'Just tell him what I said,' Henry snapped.

When Gabriel translated what Henry wanted, the old man very nearly *did* burst a gasket. He started shouting at the two prospectors, and all the other men began shouting, too.

*BANG!*

Henry's pistol was pointing straight up at the sky. A whisp of blue smoke curled out of its barrel.

The Indians fell silent. It was probably the first time many of them had heard a firearm. Pistols are *loud*. Even my ears were ringing, and I was 30 metres away.

'Tell the old man to give us the stick,' Henry said.

But still the old man refused to give it up.

Bernard drew his pistol and aimed it at the ground, just a few centimetres from the old man's bare feet. *BANG!* An explosion of dirt and leaves sprayed up into the Indian's startled face. He looked down, wide-eyed, at the small round hole in the middle of the track.

'Tell him,' Bernard said to Gabriel, 'zat ze next hole vill be in his foot.'

This time the old man saw sense. The *garimpeiros'* weapons were too loud and dangerous. Scowling, he handed the ceremonial club to Henry.

'Sank you,' said Bernard. He waved his pistol menacingly at the Indians. 'Everyone go back to your village now. Except you,' he said, grabbing Gabriel by the arm.

'What do you want the kid for?' Henry asked.

'For insurance,' said Bernard. He smiled at Gabriel. 'Tell zem no one vill be following us. If anyone follows, a bad thing vill happen to you.'

When Gabriel translated Bernard's threat to the grim-faced Indians, the boy's father stepped to the front of the group and dropped the glass necklace in the middle of the track. Several of the other men threw their Chupa Chups on the ground. I was glad none of them had brought weapons with them. They looked angry enough to start a war. But their blowguns would have been no match for the *garimpeiros'* pistols.

'Go!' Bernard barked, firing another shot into the air.

One by one, the Indians turned and disappeared up the track towards their village. Gabriel's father was the last to go. Just before he turned away, his sharp hunter's gaze shifted from the two white men who held his son hostage to the dense wall of jungle beside the track. For a moment he looked right at me.

And gave a tiny nod.

# 17
# A DEAL

I didn't know what the nod meant. Was Gabriel's father simply letting me know that he'd seen me? Or was he passing on a message? *Save my son.*

Whether or not that's what he wanted, I was going to try. He and Gabriel had saved *me*. And it was my boot prints that had led the two *garimpeiros* to their village.

As soon as the Indians had gone, Henry used a pocket knife to cut the bindings that secured the massive diamond to the end of the club. He held it up to the light.

'You beautiful, beautiful thing!' he said in a soft, awed voice. He sounded like Smeagol in *Lord of the Rings*.

'Did you see ze look in zeir eyes ven I fire my gun?'

laughed Bernard as he hoisted the heavy pack back onto his shoulders.

It was the look in Gabriel's eyes that he should have been noticing. They darted from side to side. He was about to make a break for it.

'Oh no, you don't!' said Henry, putting his foot out.

Gabriel tripped and went sprawling on the ground.

Bernard dragged him roughly to his feet and thrust his pistol between the boy's skinny shoulder blades. 'Stay in front of me vere I can see you,' he ordered.

They disappeared down the narrow track – Henry leading, then Gabriel, then Bernard holding his pistol. I waited about half a minute, then I crept out of the jungle and set off after them.

So far I had no plan other than to follow the two white men and their young Yanomami hostage. I knew where they were heading. The Matatoro River was the only way in and out of that isolated corner of the Amazon Basin. They must have a boat. It would be back at the river, pulled up on the bank or tied to a tree. As soon as they reached it, the prospectors-turned-diamond-thieves would set off downstream. I wasn't worried about them getting away with the diamond – it was only a rock – but I was very worried about Gabriel. Henry and Bernard were ruthless men. Unconsciously, I quickened my pace. It was a mistake. Because when I walked around the next corner, I nearly ran into them.

Bernard spun around and pointed the pistol straight at me. 'Vell, vell, vell, look who is here,' he said.

'H-hi!' I stammered, lowering the scalpel.

Henry put a big hand on Gabriel's shoulder so he wouldn't try anything while Bernard's back was turned. 'We thought you'd gone on ahead of us, Sam.'

My brain was racing. 'I needed a drink,' I said. 'There's a creek back there – just off to the side where you can't see it from the track.'

As soon as I said it, I remembered I was carrying Gabriel's water gourd in my left hand – a dead giveaway that I was lying.

Henry's eyes moved from the water gourd to the scalpel. 'And what's the knife for?'

'In case of jaguars.'

'Or in case you meet any big nasty men who you sink are not butterfly collectors?' suggested Bernard.

It was pointless pretending any longer. We all knew what was going on. 'I'll do a deal,' I said.

'You're in no position to do a deal,' said Henry.

'I could make you rich.'

He narrowed his eyes. 'What are you talking about?'

Burrowing into one of my pockets, I pulled out the big lump of gold.

'Let me see zat,' snapped Bernard

I tossed it to him. 'There's lots more where that came from.'

The tall prospector bounced the gold in the palm of his hand, feeling the weight of it. 'Vere did you get zis?'

'I can show you,' I said. 'But there are three conditions.'

Bernard tossed the gold to Henry. 'As ve said, troublemaker, you are in no position for making deals.'

But I was watching Henry. The greedy, Smeagol-look was back in his eyes as he examined the gold.

'I can make you the richest men in the world,' I said. 'What you're holding is just the tip of the iceberg. There's lots more where it came from – tonnes and tonnes of gold.'

Henry gave a little laugh. 'You're exaggerating.'

'I'm not. See its flat edges? They were made by a tomahawk. I had to chop it out of a gold nugget as big as a house.'

Henry and Bernard exchanged doubtful looks. But they were prospectors – no prospector could turn down a chance to get his hands on so much gold.

'What are your conditions?' asked Henry.

I caught Gabriel's eye. He looked as scared as a deer. 'First, I want you to let Gabriel go.'

'You sink ve are fools?' Bernard sneered. 'If ve don't haff a hostage, the Indians vill come after us.'

'Not if you give Gabriel the diamond to take back to them.'

'*Give him the diamond?!*' the two prospectors cried together.

'That's my second condition,' I said. 'The diamond belongs to Gabriel's people. If you give it back, they'll have no reason to come after us.'

Henry shook his head. 'You're asking us to give away a diamond that's worth at least a million dollars.'

'I'm asking you to give it *back*,' I corrected him.

'And what's a million dollars in comparison to a gold nugget as big as a house?'

The two prospectors exchanged another look.

'Vot is your third condition?' Bernard asked.

'That we be partners.'

Bernard raised one eyebrow. 'You are forgetting who has ze guns.'

'And *you're* forgetting who knows where the gold is,' I reminded him. 'I found it, so it's only fair that I get a share of the profits.'

Henry laughed. 'You've got spunk, sonny, I'll say that for you,' he said. He turned to Bernard. 'What say we give him ten per cent?'

'Not enough,' I said. 'There are three of us, so we should split it three ways. I want 33 and a third per cent.'

Henry sighed and held out his hand. 'You drive a hard bargain, Sam, but you've got yourself a deal.'

# 18
# GROWWWWWWL!

We walked in single file down the track. Henry and Bernard had agreed to my conditions – well, sort of. Gabriel was still with us and they still had the diamond. They said they'd release him – and give up the diamond – once I'd led them to the giant gold nugget. They didn't trust me. And I didn't trust them. We were partners in name only. I had simply come up with the partner idea to make them think I was like them – that getting rich was what I cared about most. But I cared more about staying alive, and keeping the silent promise I'd made to Gabriel's father.

So far I had succeeded.

The prospectors pretended Gabriel and I weren't prisoners. They had put their pistols away. But it only takes a couple of seconds to pull a pistol out of its holster. They were keeping a close eye on us. I was in the lead, then Henry, then Gabriel, then Bernard. Henry had taken the folding scalpel and put it in his pack.

'For safekeeping,' he'd said. They weren't taking any chances.

But we were in the Amazon jungle – just *being there* meant taking chances.

We came to a place where the ground was badly trampled. I recognised a tree with huge leaves like elephants' ears. Twenty metres past it, I spied what I was looking for – a smear of blood across a fallen branch and drag-marks leading into the jungle.

'We go down this trail now,' I said, veering suddenly off the track.

'I don't see a trail,' Henry said suspiciously.

'It becomes more obvious further along.'

I ducked and weaved further into the tangled undergrowth. The prospectors had no choice but to follow. They sounded like a pair of buffalos. Their huge packs snagged on every branch and vine. Their sneakers crunched leaves and snapped sticks. Gabriel, with his small frame and bare feet, made no noise at all. I hoped he would realise what I was doing and be ready for what lay ahead. I was taking a huge risk.

'Are you sure zis is correct vay?' asked Bernard.

I passed a spot of blood on a grass stalk. My heart was in my mouth. 'I'm sure,' I said softly. 'It's somewhere along here.'

Part of me hoped I wasn't going to find what I was looking for.

'This is beginning to feel like a wild goose chase,' puffed Henry.

*Not a wild goose chase,* said a scared little voice in my head, *a wild* puma *chase.*

*GROWWWWWWWL!*

I was ready for it – and hopefully Gabriel was, too – but Henry and Bernard were taken completely by surprise. One of them let out a yell of panic, the other screamed. They got such a fright, they didn't even think of using their pistols, but went crashing back through the jungle like a buffalo stampede.

I stayed where I was, too frightened to move.

Part of my brain wondered where Gabriel was, but I dared not turn my head even a millimetre to look for him. I was practically standing on the puma. But that wasn't the worst bit.

I was standing *in* its dinner!

The undergrowth was so thick I'd blundered onto the dead peccary before I'd seen it. My right foot had disappeared all the way up to the ankle inside the half-eaten carcass.

Gross! In normal circumstances, I would have thrown up. But when your life's on the line, you react differently.

'Stay calm,' I said softly, speaking to myself as much as to the crouching puma as I lifted my blood-smeared boot out of the dead peccary's rib cage. 'Nobody's going to get hurt.'

Just as I'd hoped, the puma had been feasting for a couple of hours and its belly was bloated with fresh meat. The last thing it wanted was trouble. It didn't move a muscle as I backed slowly away into the jungle.

Only when I was out of sight of the big cat did I start shaking. My legs felt like jelly and I almost *did* throw up. But I managed to control myself. I had to keep a clear head. So far my daring plan had worked. Thanks to the puma, I'd escaped from Henry and Bernard. But they weren't far away.

And they were looking for me.

'VERE ARE YOU, SAM?' Bernard shouted from the direction of the track.

Giving the puma a wide berth, I crept the other way.

Then Henry shouted, 'SAM! GABRIEL! ARE YOU BOYS ALL RIGHT?'

They were looking for Gabriel, too. Like me, he must have escaped when the prospectors panicked. I hoped he would have the good sense to lie low for a while, then sneak back to his village when the coast was clear.

'COME BACK, SAM!' yelled Henry.

'VE HAFF A DEAL!' yelled Bernard.

They must have known I wasn't coming back. A deal doesn't count when it's made at gunpoint. Now that Gabriel and I were free, the deal was off.

But we still had some unfinished business.

# 19
# WHOMP!

I had an idea

The prospectors had taken my lump of gold, so I'd take their boat. It seemed like a fair exchange.

If I had a boat, I could go looking for Uncle Shaun and Caesar. We could use it to travel down the river. Then we'd send back a rescue party to collect the prospectors – in a police boat.

But I didn't think Henry and Bernard would take kindly to my idea. They wouldn't just hand over their boat. And they were armed and dangerous. So I had to get to the river before them.

But how could I get to the river ahead of the

prospectors? The track was the only way to the river, and they were on the track.

Then I remembered what Henry had said earlier about a wild goose chase. It means going looking for something that isn't there.

Bingo!

I would lead Henry and Bernard on another wild goose chase. One that took them deep into the jungle. Then I'd circle back to the track and race them to the river. I couldn't run very fast in Uncle Shaun's oversized boots, but the prospectors had heavy packs so they'd be much slower than me. It would give me enough time to find their boat and get away before they arrived. Or so I hoped.

'SAM, VERE ARE YOU?' shouted Bernard.

I smiled to myself. Only I knew the whereabouts of the giant gold nugget. It was a secret worth millions of dollars. So to the prospectors, *I* was worth millions of dollars. It gave me a lot of power.

'*Over here!*' I called, meshing my fingers across my mouth so I'd sound further away than I actually was. '*The puma chased me up a tree!*'

'*IS THE PUMA STILL THERE?*' Henry shouted.

'*It's right below me,*' I called through my cupped hands. I was no longer anywhere near the puma, but I wanted Henry and Bernard to think it had me bailed up in a tree. It would make them very cautious when they approached, giving me more time to circle back around them.

As silently as possible, I began creeping through the jungle at right angles to the direction the prospectors would approach from.

*BANG!*

The pistol shot was no more than 30 metres away. I got such a fright, I nearly jumped out of Uncle Shaun's size-12 boots.

'*DID THAT SCARE THE PUMA?*' shouted Henry.

I couldn't answer. It would give away my position and they would realise I'd moved. I was supposed to be trapped up a tree about 15 metres behind me.

'*VERE ARE YOU?*' Bernard called.

I dropped to my hands and knees and began crawling through the vine-choked undergrowth, directly away from the voices.

'SAM, WHAT IN BLAZES ARE YOU UP TO?' yelled Henry.

'STOP PLAYING GAMES!' shouted Bernard.

They both sounded angry. I heard them crashing through the jungle again, throwing caution to the wind as they headed towards the spot where they'd last heard my voice.

Then I heard more crashing. And the *thump, thump, thump* of galloping hooves.

Coming in my direction!

There was barely time to stand up before a huge black creature, like a cross between a cow and an elephant, burst out of the jungle and slammed into me.

*WHOMP!*

# 20
# TEETH!

The South American tapir is the largest animal in the Amazon jungle. It grows nearly as big as a horse. It's frightened of humans so it usually isn't dangerous. It will hide in dense jungle until humans go away. But if they come looking for it, or scare it with gunfire, a tapir will panic and head for water.

That's when tapirs become dangerous. Because they won't stop for anything. Not even a jaguar.

It's not a good idea to get in their way.

*WHOMP!*

The tapir hit me at about 50 kilometres per hour. It sent me flying. I landed flat on my back on the soft, muddy ground. For a few seconds I lay there, stunned, looking up at the green mass of jungle above me. My brain still hadn't quite worked out what had happened. All I knew was a huge black animal had knocked me over and now it was gone. I could hear it crashing away through the jungle somewhere behind me.

And I could hear more crashing. Coming from the other direction. Getting louder.

Then I heard voices.

'Sounds like he's running away!'

'I told you he voz a no good troublemaker!'

Henry and Bernard must have heard the big black animal and thought it was me. They were coming in my direction. I had to get out of there!

Scrambling to my feet, I set off after the tapir. It had gone ploughing off through the undergrowth like a bulldozer, leaving a narrow green tunnel in its wake. Head down to avoid the lush curtain of overhanging foliage, I slithered down a steep, ferny bank and found my escape route blocked by a stagnant, green creek. It was about ten-metres wide and clogged with floating weeds and lily pads. There was thick jungle on the other side. I could see a channel through the weeds where the tapir had crossed, but my recent close encounters with the giant anaconda and the electric eel made me nervous about going in. *Anything* could be lurking under the surface!

I hesitated at the creek's edge. A cloud of mosquitoes buzzed around my ears. Henry and Bernard were getting closer. There was no alternative. Taking a deep breath, I stepped into the creek and started wading across.

*Thump!*

Something hit me on the right ankle. Even though my ankle was protected by Uncle Shaun's thick leather boots, it felt like being struck by a small hammer.

*Thump!*

It hit me again. Same ankle, but on the other side.

What was going on?

Then – *thump!* – it hit my right toe. Only this hit was different. As well as the thump of impact, I felt something sharp. Right through the leather.

Teeth!

Through a gap in the weeds, I glimpsed a big silver-and-red fish. With teeth like a mouthful of barbed wire.

A piranha!

It wasn't alone. There were dozens of them. They were attacking my right boot – the one that had stepped into the dead peccary and got covered in blood – and tearing it to shreds.

I had to get out of the water. Fast!

'Do not take anozer step, troublemaker,' said a familiar voice behind me, 'or I shoot.'

# 21
# BAD AS SHARKS

Which would be worse? I asked myself. Being shot in the back by *garimpeiros*, or being eaten alive by piranhas?

It was no contest.

I kept wading towards the other bank, reasonably sure that Bernard and Henry wouldn't shoot me – I was worth too much to them alive.

*BANG!*

The bullet hit the water just beside my left knee, showering me with spray.

'Are you deaf, troublemaker?' roared Bernard.

I kept going. The prospector had aimed to miss, but the piranhas meant business. They were attacking both boots now. At any moment they would notice my bare legs.

*BANG!*

This time Bernard aimed just to my right. The splash was nearly as high as my head.

'I told you to *stop*!' he roared.

I scrambled out of the water on the other side of the creek and turned around. Both prospectors stood on the other bank with their pistols levelled straight at me.

'OK, I've stopped,' I said, raising both my hands in the air.

'Come back to ziss side,' snarled Bernard.

Suddenly I had a plan. 'But the gold's on *this* side,' I said.

Bernard brandished his pistol threateningly. 'Ve haff had enough of your tricks, troublemaker!'

'I'm not tricking you,' I said, looking him straight in the eye. I can be a good liar when I have to be. My life depended on them believing me.

Pointing behind the two prospectors at the tunnel through the undergrowth made by the tapir, I continued: 'I told you about the track leading to the place where

I found the gold. It crosses the creek here, then there's only a couple of hundred metres to go.'

Bernard and Henry looked back at the 'track', then at me.

'Vy did you run avay from us?' Bernard asked suspiciously.

'I wasn't running away from you,' I said, 'I was running away from the puma.'

Henry seemed doubtful. 'I thought it had you bailed up in a tree.'

'It did. But pumas can climb trees. When it came up after me, I had to jump down and make a run for it.'

Henry and Bernard glanced at each other, then slowly lowered their pistols. They'd bought it! They believed my story.

Now they were going to cross the creek.

Should I warn them? I wondered. They had threatened to kill me, and they might still kill me if I didn't get away before they discovered I wasn't leading them to the gold. But I had to say something.

'Be careful – there are piranhas.'

Both men stopped at the water's edge. Nothing was

visible through the thick layer of plant matter that covered the surface.

'*You* got across,' Henry said.

I shrugged. 'I was lucky.'

He and Bernard studied me for a moment, wondering whether or not I was lying.

'Zen ve can be lucky, too,' said Bernard.

He stepped into the water, closely followed by Henry.

Well, don't say I didn't warn you, I thought.

They weren't lucky. The smell of blood from my boots was still in the creek. The piranhas were on red alert. When the prospectors were halfway across, the water all around them began to swirl and boil and splash.

'Vot is happening?' asked Bernard, his eyes nearly popping out.

'It's piranhas!' cried Henry.

Both men drew their pistols and began firing straight down into the creek – *BANG! BANG! BANG! BANG!* – as they blundered through the foaming water towards me.

Now was my chance to escape. The prospectors were too busy fighting off the piranhas to worry about anything else.

I was out of there!

But I didn't get far. No sooner had I turned my back on the creek and rushed headlong into the jungle, than I burst out into the open again. And skidded to a standstill.

Shishkebab!

I was standing on the bank of another creek. It looked identical to the one behind me – the same murky green water, the same mat of weeds and lily pads covering it. And the same deadly welcoming committee waiting under the lily pads.

Nothing – and I mean *nothing!* – could have persuaded me to cross it.

Behind me there were two more shots, then silence. I crouched behind a tree, pressing my back against the cool mossy bark and shaking all over.

'Bloomin' heck!' Henry swore.

'Zoze horrible fish!' muttered Bernard. 'Zey are bad as sharks.'

The prospectors were just through the trees. Less than three metres of jungle separated us. Keeping my head down, I crept away at right angles along the bank of the second creek. But again I didn't get far. Twenty metres further on, the creek I was following joined *another* creek. I found myself on the narrow point of land where the two waterways met. I had no choice but to follow the bank of the third creek. It curved back at a sharp angle through the overhanging jungle.

I'd only gone a few paces when the sound of men's voices stopped me in my tracks. Dropping into a crouch, I peered cautiously through a thicket of tall, pink-stemmed reeds. Henry and Bernard were sitting at the water's edge only a few metres away.

I was back where I'd started!

What I'd mistaken for separate creeks were simply branches of the first one. It had split in two to flow around a small stand of jungle growing on a raised sandbank. When I looked past Henry and Bernard, I could see where the two arms of the creek rejoined at the other end.

We were on an island.

# 22
# TRAPPED!

I spied on the prospectors from my hiding place behind the pink reeds. Henry was sitting on his pack, wrapping a bandage around his ankle. Bernard's pack lay open beside him with a first-aid kit next to it. He had rolled up his tattered jeans and was putting on plasters. His legs looked like untidy patchwork quilts with blood seeping through the seams. It made me wince to look at them.

Both men had put their pistols back in their holsters.

'Ven I see zat troublemaker again, I don't give him another chance,' Bernard growled as he applied another plaster. 'Bang, bang!'

'Not if I see him first,' muttered Henry, securing his bandage with a safety pin.

They had finally worked out I'd been leading them on a wild goose chase. I had to get off the island before they found me.

But the island was surrounded by ravenous piranhas.

I was trapped!

Or maybe I wasn't. I hadn't explored the other end of the island yet. There might be a fallen tree or some rocks I could use as stepping stones.

Henry and Bernard still had some first aid to do. It meant I'd have a few minutes before they came looking for me. Backing away from the reeds, I crept into the jungle and crossed to the other side of the island. Then I followed the shore back in the other direction. The island was very narrow – halfway along I passed within three metres of the prospectors. It was pretty scary. If I rustled some ferns or stepped on a brittle stick, it would give the game away. I wished it *was* a game, rather than a desperate attempt to stay alive. I could still hear Bernard's voice in my head – *Ven I see zat troublemaker again, I don't give him another chance. Bang, bang!*

I remembered other bangs, too – the ones made by their pistols – and that got me thinking . . .

When I reached the other end of the island, my hopes of finding an escape route quickly vanished. There were no fallen trees and no stepping stones. If anything, the creek – both arms of it – was wider at this end.

Which meant, I suddenly thought, the water was probably not as deep!

If I splashed across flat out, I might get to the other side before the piranhas even knew I was coming.

For a few seconds it seemed like a workable plan. Until I glimpsed a flicker of movement beneath one of the lily pads. It was a fin. When I looked closely, I saw a big, saw-toothed fish hanging in the shadow of the lily pad. A piranha. It was watching me. Now that I knew what to look for, I spotted more of them. They lurked under every lily pad. Hundreds of piranhas. All of them were watching me. Watching and waiting. Only their fins moved as they waited for their next meal.

But I wasn't going to be it.

Suddenly there was a flurry of movement. Piranhas zoomed left and right, leaving an empty space between two lily pads. My skin pricked as a long, greyish-green shape rose to the surface and gulped a big mouthful of air, then slowly sank back down into the shadows.

Here's something I didn't know – electric eels breathe.

I noticed how the piranhas had made room for it when it came up for air. That gave me an idea.

There was another stand of pink reeds growing at the edge of the jungle behind me. I found one that was half-broken near the roots. It was as thick as my finger and as tough as bamboo. As quietly as possible, I wriggled it back and forth until it came free. Then I wormed my way into the jungle, knelt down and emptied my pockets.

# 23
# MAKE MY DAY

I crouched over the broken reed and carefully peeled the back off an adhesive dressing. Heavy footsteps came crunching along the creek bank. I paused briefly from my work, holding my breath as Henry and Bernard limped past my leafy hiding spot. A minute later they went past on the other side, going in the opposite direction.

'The vater goes right around,' Bernard muttered.

'It's an island,' said Henry.

'How vill ve get off?'

'I don't know. The creek's teeming with piranhas. We're trapped.'

As I listened to their footsteps move away, I wondered

how long it would take the prospectors to work out that they weren't the only ones who were trapped on the island.

I wasn't left wondering for long.

'TROUBLEMAKER, VERE ARE YOU?' Bernard called from the other end of the island.

For about a minute there was silence. Then I heard a stick snap.

'WE KNOW YOU'RE HERE SOMEWHERE!' shouted Henry.

There was more crackling and crunching in the undergrowth. It slowly grew louder. So did Henry's and Bernard's voices.

'IT'S NO USE HIDING, SAM.'

'COME OUT, COME OUT, VEREVER YOU ARE!'

A shiver passed through me. I knew what they were doing. They were systematically searching the island from one end to the other. It was only a matter of time before they found me. Applying a final touch to my secret weapon, I wriggled out of my hiding place and ran back to the spot where I'd seen the electric eel.

But all I saw were piranhas.

I stood at the water's edge, trying to ignore the

prospectors' taunting calls as I strained my eyes to see into the shady green water. It didn't help that the sun was going down and daylight was rapidly fading.

I was so intent on watching the creek that I didn't see the small brown figure emerge from the jungle on the other side.

'Sam!'

It was Gabriel.

'Stay out of the creek – it's swarming with piranhas,' I warned in a hushed voice. My eyes searched the shadowy jungle behind him. 'Where are the others?'

Gabriel came down to the water's edge. 'What others?'

'I thought you'd gone back to your village to get help.'

'I hide from *garimpeiros*, then I come to find you,' Gabriel whispered.

He needn't have whispered, because the *garimpeiros* were right behind me.

'Vot haff ve here?' said Bernard, limping out of the shadows with his pistol drawn. 'Both ze troublemakers.'

Henry came hobbling along behind him, holding his pistol, too. Neither man was wearing his pack.

'Go and get help, Gabriel,' I said.

Bernard pointed his pistol across the creek. 'Stay right vere you are, little boy.'

I was 99 per cent sure his pistol wasn't loaded. I'd counted the shots. Both men had revolvers – six-shooters – and 12 shots had been fired that afternoon.

But what if I was wrong? I might have miscounted. Or the prospectors might have reloaded their pistols after crossing the creek. I couldn't gamble with Gabriel's life.

Here goes nothing, I thought. And darted straight towards Bernard and Henry.

It was the last thing they expected. They both swung their pistols around, trying to keep me in their sights, as I ran right between them.

*Click! Click!*

Luckily for the prospectors, I'd counted correctly. If their pistols had been loaded, they probably would have missed me and shot each other!

'Get help, Gabriel!' I yelled over my shoulder, as I ran flat out around the edge of the island.

I had a head start on Henry and Bernard, and both prospectors were limping badly from their piranha bites. Sticking to the shoreline, where there was no jungle to slow me down, I sprinted around the edge of the island. Just as I'd hoped, the prospectors' packs lay on the creek bank where I'd last seen them. I picked one up and heaved it as far as I could out over the piranha-infested water.

But just as I lifted the second one, Bernard came crashing through the ferns and grabbed the other end of it.

'Let it go!' he snarled, trying to pull it away from me.

For a few seconds we had a tug of war. Bernard was bigger than me and much stronger. He turned me in a circle, then started pushing me backwards towards the creek.

'Now I give you a taste of your own medicine, troublemaker!' He grimaced.

The grimace was his downfall. Because it reminded me of his weakness. I lashed out with one foot. *Thump!* Uncle Shaun's big, heavy boot hit him squarely on one of his patchwork-quilt legs. Bernard's eyes nearly doubled in size and he let out a howl of pain. Before he could recover, I wrenched the pack out of his hands and twisted away from him. The pack swung in a big circle.

I twirled it three times, like a hammer-thrower at the Olympics, then let fly.

It sailed across the creek and splashed into the water only a metre from the other shore.

'I vill kill you!' Bernard muttered, drawing his pistol from its holster.

But he wasn't going to kill anyone. Because a pistol without ammunition is useless. The spare bullets – if there were any – were in one of the packs. And I'd got rid of the packs.

Realising I'd outsmarted him, Bernard swung his pistol like a club. I jumped out of the way. He came lurching after me, his breath heaving, his face contorted in rage. But his injuries made him slow. It was easy to stay out of reach. I led him in circles. Finally, in frustration, Bernard hurled the pistol at me. I ducked. It flew over my head and landed with a splash in the creek behind me.

Henry arrived moments later, hobbling like a 100-year-old man. When he saw me, he raised his pistol and pulled the trigger.

*Click!*

His face turned bright red. He turned to Bernard.

'Where are the bullets?'

Bernard didn't say anything. He simply pointed at the two packs lying in the shallow water on the other side of the creek.

When Henry saw what I'd done, he dropped his pistol and hobbled towards me with his hands balled into fists. Bernard came limping from the other direction.

I picked up a broken branch and held it out in front of me with two hands, like it was a ju-jitsu fighting stick. 'If either of you come close,' I warned, 'I'll whack you on the legs.'

Both men stopped in their tracks. Bernard looked down at his legs. Fresh blood was seeping through the bandages. Without a word, he turned and sat down on a log.

Henry's eyes were narrowed to slits. If looks could kill, I'd be dead. But I met his chilling stare with a glare of my own.

A glare that said, *Go ahead, make my day!*

And I waved the stick at him.

Henry slowly lowered his arms. His fists unclenched. Then he sank down on the log next to Bernard.

'You win, Sam Fox,' he muttered.

That was when we heard Gabriel scream.

# 24
# ZAP!

I don't remember running back to the other end of the island. I just remember getting there. And seeing Gabriel dangling over the creek. He clung to a skinny green vine. Below him, the water boiled and splashed with a thousand blood-crazed piranhas.

'Help me!' he cried.

The vine was too thin and slippery to climb. It hung from a tree that sloped out from the other bank. Gabriel must have tried to swing across to the island but he'd misjudged the distance.

'Hold on,' I said.

My secret weapon lay where I'd dropped it when Henry

and Bernard had tried to shoot me with their empty pistols. I picked it up and peered into the water.

'I going to fall,' Gabriel whimpered.

He was losing his grip. His small, knotted hands started sliding slowly down the vine. The piranhas saw him getting closer and went into a frenzy of excitement. They began leaping into the air, jaws snapping like rat-traps as they tried to latch onto his dangling bare feet.

'Pull your feet up,' I said, still watching the water.

Gabriel drew his legs up out of the way. But his hands were still slipping. Centimetre by centimetre, he was getting closer to the piranhas' snapping jaws.

'Help me, Sam!'

'I will help you,' I promised. In my raised right hand, I held the two-metre-long reed I'd fashioned into a spear. Taped to its business end with adhesive dressings was my EpiPen. 'Hang in there for a few more seconds, Gabriel.'

I'd seen what I was waiting for. Rising to the surface at the edge of the piranha frenzy was a smooth, greyish-green head.

'Can't hang on!' shrieked Gabriel.

With a final, despairing scream, he let go.

And I hurled my spear.

Bullseye!

An EpiPen is like a hypodermic needle. It contains adrenaline. The electric eel got a full dose. It went hyper. And turned on the power. Six hundred volts.

*ZAP!*

It was like an underwater bomb going off. A circular ripple fizzed out across the surface and about a thousand piranhas leapt out of the water, all at the same time. Some landed on giant lily pads and lay there with their ugly mouths wide-open. Others splashed back into the water and went belly-up. I had never seen so many dead or stunned fish.

But it was Gabriel I was worried about. He'd hit the water about half a second after the power surge, and disappeared beneath the dark surface.

My rescue attempt had backfired. Instead of saving him, I'd got him electrocuted.

Throwing all caution to the wind, I waded out through the lifeless, floating piranhas, feeling like a murderer.

I'd killed Gabriel!

The water bubbled, a lily pad flopped to one side, and

up bobbed a little brown figure. It was Gabriel. He was alive! But he looked terrified. When I tried to put my arms around him, he climbed me like a tree.

'It's OK, Gabriel,' I said, hugging his small, shivering body. He was no bigger than Harry and Jordan, my five-year-old twin brothers. 'The piranhas are all dead.'

I was wrong. No sooner had I spoken, than a wave of fins came weaving towards us through the lifeless, floating bodies of their fellow fish. The piranhas that were too far away to be killed by the electric eel's shock wave were coming to clean up the dead. And us, too, if we didn't get out of the creek in a hurry.

With Gabriel clutched in my arms, I waded across to the far shore. We made it just before the new wave of piranhas arrived. One latched onto the heel of my boot as I staggered out of the creek. It didn't let go until I was halfway up the bank. I kicked it back into the water and lowered Gabriel to the ground.

He looked up at me and smiled. 'You are very brave warrior, Sam.'

I didn't feel brave, I felt scared. It was nearly dark and we were surrounded by jungle. *Amazon* jungle.

Not a good place to be at night.

I led Gabriel along the creek bank until we were opposite the two prospectors. They hadn't moved since I'd last seen them. They still sat on the log, hugging their legs and looking sorry for themselves.

'How did you get across the creek?' Henry asked.

'That would be telling,' I said.

Their packs bobbed in the water only a metre or two from our shore. Gabriel and I used sticks to drag them up onto the bank. I rummaged through them until I found the stolen diamond, and gave it to Gabriel to take back to the old man. I found my lump of gold, too, and slipped it into my pocket.

'Can ve have some vater?' Bernard asked.

There was a big water bottle attached to each pack. I kept one for Gabriel and me, then walked down to the edge of the creek.

'I'll do a swap,' I said. I had found a box of bullets in one of the packs. 'This bottle of water for Henry's pistol.'

The prospectors had no choice but to agree. They needed water, and drinking from the creek was out of the question. As soon as we had made the exchange,

I loaded the big pistol and pointed it up into the air.

*BANG!*

'Why you do that?' Gabriel asked.

I felt embarrassed. 'To scare away jaguars,' I said.

So much for being a brave warrior.

It was fully dark now and we didn't have torches to find our way back to the track. Gabriel and I would have to stay where we were until daylight, or risk getting hopelessly lost. We could have spent the night in a tree, but it was too dark to find one that I could climb – anyway, jaguars and pumas can climb trees. Instead, we wrapped ourselves in a groundsheet from one of the packs and made ourselves comfortable with our backs to a wall of small palms.

*BANG!*

A pistol shot every so often would frighten anything away. I had lots of bullets.

The last thing I expected was to *attract* something with the pistol. But that's what happened.

After my third or fourth shot, I heard a rustling noise, then the snap of a stick breaking. Gabriel gripped my arm.

'Something coming!' he whispered.

Hooley dooly! We stood up, letting the groundsheet fall to the ground as we backed down to the water's edge. I pointed the loaded pistol away from me and peered into the inky blackness.

Then there was another rustling sound, closer this time.

'Wh-who's there?' I stammered.

Suddenly I was blinded by torchlight.

'Sam?'

'Uncle Shaun?!'

# 25
# LUNGS OF THE WORLD

Here's what had happened. After I got swept away in the peke-peke, Uncle Shaun and Caesar made it ashore and set off after me along the riverbank. But the jungle was very thick and it took them nearly two hours to reach the Big Beast. When they found the capsized peke-peke caught in a snag about 50 metres below the waterfall, they feared the worst – either I'd drowned in the river, or been killed when I went over the falls. But then something weird happened. An arrow fell out of the sky and plopped into the river not ten metres from where they were standing. Uncle Shaun recognised the orange feathers. It was one of his crossbow arrows (the one

Gabriel's father shot at the rat-like animal) and it seemed to have come from the other side of the river.

Was I alive, after all?

It was no use shouting because the waterfall was so loud, so Uncle Shaun and Caesar set about crossing the river to look for me. First they had to free the peke-peke from the snag and repair a big hole at the back where the outboard motor had been ripped off. It took nearly an hour. While they were doing it, Henry and Bernard came puttering along the other side of the river in their own peke-peke. Uncle Shaun and Caesar tried to attract their attention, but again the waterfall made shouting useless and the overhanging trees largely hid them from the prospectors' view.

By the time Uncle Shaun and Caesar had repaired their peke-peke and crossed the river, the prospectors had dragged their own canoe up the bank and disappeared into the jungle. Uncle Shaun wasn't sure whether to follow them or not. He thought I'd be more likely to stay near the river than go traipsing off into the jungle. Then Caesar thought he heard a gunshot (probably Bernard trying to scare the puma). A while later there was a whole volley of shots (when the prospectors were crossing the creek) and this time Uncle Shaun heard them, too.

'I'll bet Sam's got something to do with that,' he said.

The afternoon was well advanced by then, so they borrowed a torch from the bundle of supplies left in the prospectors' peke-peke and set off into the jungle to investigate. It grew dark and they were about to abandon their search, when there was another gunshot, much louder than the earlier ones (me trying to scare away jaguars). It was followed at ten minute intervals by a series of gunshots that eventually led Uncle Shaun and Caesar right to me.

But that wasn't the end of my Amazon adventure.

The following day I was made an honorary member of the Yanomami tribe. Gabriel's great uncle, the old man who owned the diamond, was also the village leader. He placed a string of red feathers around my neck and gave me a new name, *Nabebe*.

Then there was a big feast held in our honour. The whole village attended, as well as Uncle Shaun, Caesar and me. There were many sorts of strange food and all of it was delicious, but I was careful not to eat any meat.

When we were leaving, Gabriel and his father presented me with a blowgun and six darts – without poison tips.

'Father say thank you.'

Early the next morning, I finally saw a jaguar. We had just pulled out from shore in the prospectors' peke-peke, towing ours behind us on a long rope with Henry and Bernard aboard. Neither of them had objected to swapping boats, they were just grateful to be leaving the jungle behind. In exchange for not reporting them to the police, both prospectors had promised to leave Brazil on the next flight out – and never return.

'Look, Sam – a jaguar.'

I looked where Uncle Shaun was pointing. The big spotted cat stood proudly on the rocks above the waterfall, watching us go chugging off down the Matatoro River.

'You are very lucky to see a jaguar, Mr Sam,' said Caesar. 'They are very rare.'

'And getting rarer,' Uncle Shaun said.

He explained how global warming and logging were destroying the jungle. 'The trees of the Amazon rainforest are the lungs of the world,' he said. 'They take carbon dioxide out of the air and make it fit for humans to breathe. If we cut down all the trees, it won't only affect the animals and birds, it will affect the whole human race.'

It was pretty scary. And it got me thinking.

'Uncle Shaun,' I said, slipping my hand into my pocket, 'you know how Henry and Bernard were looking for diamonds and gold and stuff. What if someone *did* find gold here, and started a gold mine? Would they have to cut down many trees?'

Uncle Shaun looked grim. 'Millions,' he said. 'There wouldn't just be a gold mine, there'd be trucks, roads, drains running into the river, pollution. Eventually there might even be a town and an airfield. Environmentally, it would be a complete disaster.'

I'd known all along that Uncle Shaun didn't like prospectors. That's why I hadn't told him about the gold. Only Henry and Bernard knew. But they didn't know where I'd found it. And if they broke their word and came back up the river looking, they'd never find it. The Big Beast would keep its secret.

The lump of gold was heavy in my hand. Running my fingers over its cold, hard surface, I looked back one last time. The jaguar had disappeared. But right below the waterfall, a long glistening shape rose out of the foaming water like the head and neck of a mythical sea monster. I got goose bumps all over. The giant anaconda was 200 metres from the peke-peke – too far away for me to see its eyes – but I could swear it was watching me.

'I won't tell anyone,' I whispered.

Dipping my hand into the river, I let the gold slip from my fingers.